Little Lord Fauntleroy [abridged]: Für den Schulgebrauch bearbeitet

Frances Hodgson Burnett

CHAPTER I.

A GREAT SURPRISE.

Cedric himself knew nothing whatever about it. It had never been even mentioned to him. He knew that his papa had been an Englishman, because his mamma had told him so; but then his papa had died when he was so little a boy that he could not remember very much about him, except that he was big, and had blue eyes and a long moustache, and that it was a splendid thing to be carried around the room on his shoulder. Since his papa's death, Cedric had found out that it was best not to talk to his mamma about him. When his father was ill, Cedric had been sent away, and when he had returned, everything was over; and his mother, who had been very ill, too, was only just beginning to sit in her chair by the window. She was pale and thin, and all the dimples had gone from her pretty face, and her eyes looked large and mournful, and she was dressed in black.

He and his mamma knew very few people, and lived what might have been thought very lonely lives, although Cedric did not know it was lonely until he grew older and heard why it was they had no visitors. Then he was told that his mamma was an orphan, and quite alone in the world when his papa had married her. Their marriage brought them the ill-will of several persons. The one who was most angry of all, however, was the Captain's father, who lived in England, and was a very rich and important old nobleman, with a very bad temper, and a very violent dislike to America and Americans. He had two sons older than Captain Cedric; and it was the law that the elder of these sons should inherit the family title and estates, which were very rich and splendid; if the eldest son died the next one would be heir; so though he was a member of such a great family, there was little chance that Captain Cedric would be very rich himself.

But it so happened that Nature had given to the younger son gifts which she had not bestowed upon his elder brothers. He had a beautiful face and a fine, strong, graceful figure; he had a bright smile and a sweet, gay voice; he was brave and generous, and had the kindest heart in the world, and seemed to have the power to make every one love him. But it was not so with his elder brothers; neither of them was handsome, or kind, or clever; they cared nothing for study, and wasted both time and money, and made few real friends. The old Earl, their father, was constantly disappointed and humiliated by them; his heir was no honour to his noble name. It was very bitter, the old Earl thought, that the son who was only third, should be the one who had all the gifts, and all the charms. Sometimes he almost hated the handsome young man because he seemed to have the good things which should have gone with the stately title and the magnificent estates. It was in one of his fits of petulance that he sent him off to travel in America.

But after about six months, he began to feel lonely, and longed in secret to see his son again, so he wrote to Captain Cedric and ordered him home. The letter he wrote crossed on its way a letter the Captain had just written to his father telling of his love for the pretty American girl, and of his intended marriage; and when the Earl received that letter, he was furiously angry. Bad as his temper was, he had never given way to it in his life as he gave way to it when he read the Captain's letter. For an hour he raged like a tiger, and then he sat down and wrote to his son, and ordered him never to come near his old home, nor to write to his father or brothers again.

The Captain was very sad when he read the letter; he was very fond of England, and he dearly loved the beautiful home where he had been born; he had even loved his ill-tempered old father; but he knew he need expect no kindness from him in the future. At first he scarcely knew what to do; he had not been brought up to work, and had no business experience, but he had courage and plenty of determination. So he sold his commission in the English army, and after some trouble found a situation in New York, and married. The change from his old life in England was very great, but he was young and happy and he hoped that hard work would do great things for him in the future. He had a small house in a quiet street, and his little boy was born there. Though he was born in so quiet and cheap a little home, it seemed as if there never had been a more fortunate baby. In the first place, he was always well, and so he never gave any one trouble; in the second place he had so sweet a temper and ways so charming that he was a pleasure to every one; and in the third place he was so beautiful to look at that he was quite a picture.

When he was old enough to walk out with his nurse, he was so handsome and strong and rosy that he attracted every one's attention, and his nurse would come home and tell his mamma stories of the ladies who had stopped their carriages to look at and speak to him, and of how pleased they were when he talked to them in his cheerful little way, as if he had known them always. His greatest charm was this cheerful, fearless, quaint little way of making friends with people.

As he grew older, he had a great many quaint little ways which amused and interested people greatly. He was so much of a companion for his mother that she scarcely cared for any other. They used to walk together and talk together and play together. When he was quite a little fellow he learned to read; and after that he used to lie on the hearth-rug, in the evening, and read aloud—sometimes stories, and sometimes big books such as older people read, and sometimes even the newspaper; and often at such times Mary, in the kitchen, would hear Mrs. Errol laughing with delight at the quaint things he said.

Mary was very fond of him, and very proud of him, too. She had been with his mother ever since he was born; and, after his father's death, had been cook and housemaid and nurse and everything else.

"Ristycratic, is it?" she would say. "It's like a young lord he looks."

Cedric did not know that he looked like a young lord; he did not know what a lord was. His greatest friend was the groceryman at the corner. His name was Mr. Hobbs, and Cedric admired and respected him very much. He thought him a very rich and powerful person, he had so many things in his store—prunes and figs and oranges and biscuits,— and he had a horse and waggon. Cedric was fond of the milkman and the baker and the apple-woman, but he liked Mr. Hobbs best of all, and was on terms of such intimacy with him that he went to see him every day, and often sat with him quite a long time discussing the topics of the hour. It was quite surprising how many things they found to talk about—the Fourth of July, for instance. When they began to talk about the Fourth of July there really seemed no end to it. Mr. Hobbs had a very bad opinion of "the British," and he told the whole story of the Revolution, relating very wonderful and patriotic stories about the villainy of the enemy and the bravery of the Revolutionary heroes, and he even generously repeated part of the Declaration of Independence. Cedric was so excited that his eyes shone and he could hardly wait to eat his dinner after he went home, he was so anxious to tell his mamma. It was, perhaps, Mr. Hobbs who gave him his first interest in politics. Mr. Hobbs was fond of reading the newspapers, and so Cedric heard a great deal about what was going on in Washington; and Mr. Hobbs would tell him whether the President was doing his duty or not.

When Cedric was between seven and eight years old, the very strange thing happened which made so wonderful a change in his life. It was quite curious, too, that the day it happened he had been talking to Mr. Hobbs about England and the Queen, and Mr. Hobbs had said some very severe things about the aristocracy, being specially indignant against earls and marquises.

They were in the midst of their conversation, when Mary appeared. Cedric thought she had come to buy some sugar, perhaps, but she had not. She looked almost pale and as if she were excited about something.

"Come home, darlint," she said; "the mistress is wantin' yez."

Cedric slipped down from his stool.

"Does she want me to go out with her, Mary?" he asked. "Good morning, Mr. Hobbs. I'll see you again."

When he reached his own house there was a coupé standing before the door, and some one was in the little parlour talking to his mamma. Mary hurried him up stairs and put on his best summer suit of cream-coloured flannel with the red scarf around the waist, and combed out his curly locks.

When he was dressed, he ran down stairs and went into the parlour. A tall, thin old gentleman with a sharp face was sitting in an arm-chair. His mother was standing near by with a pale face, and he saw that there were tears in her eyes.

"Oh, Ceddie!" she cried out, and ran to her little boy and caught him in her arms and kissed him in a little frightened, troubled way. "Oh, Ceddie, darling!"

The tall old gentleman rose from his chair and looked at Cedric with his sharp eyes. He rubbed his thin chin with his bony hand as he looked.

He seemed not at all displeased.

"And so," he said at last, slowly,—"and so this is little Lord Fauntleroy."

CHAPTER II.

CEDRIC'S FRIENDS.

There was never a more amazed little boy than Cedric during the week that followed; there was never so strange or so unreal a week. In the first place, the story his mamma told him was a very curious one. He was obliged to hear it two or three times before he could understand it. He could not imagine what Mr. Hobbs would think of it. It began with earls; his grandpapa, whom he had never seen, was an earl; and his eldest uncle, if he had not been killed by a fall from his horse, would have been an earl, too, in time; and after his death, his other uncle would have been an earl, if he had not died suddenly, in Rome, of a fever. After that, his own papa, if he had lived, would have been an earl; but since they all had died and only Cedric was left, it appeared that he was to be an earl after his grandpapa's death—and for the present he was Lord Fauntleroy.

He turned quite pale when he was first told of it.

"Oh! Dearest!" he said, "I should rather not be an earl. None of the boys are earls. Can't I not be one?"

But it seemed to be unavoidable. And when, that evening, they sat together by the open window looking out into the shabby street, he and his mother had a long talk about it. Cedric sat on his footstool, clasping one knee in his favourite attitude and wearing a bewildered little face rather red from the exertion of thinking. His grandfather had sent for him to come to England, and his mamma thought he must go.

"Because," she said, looking out of the window with sorrowful eyes, "I know your papa would wish it to be so, Ceddie. I should be a selfish little mother if I did not send you. When you are a man you will see why."

Ceddie shook his head mournfully. "I shall be very sorry to leave Mr. Hobbs," he said.

When Mr. Havisham—who was the family lawyer of the Earl of Dorincourt, and who had been sent by him to bring Lord Fauntleroy to England—came the next day, Cedric heard many things. But, somehow, it did not console him to hear that he was to be a very rich man when he grew up, and that he would have castles here and castles there, and great parks and deep mines and grand estates and tenantry. He was troubled about his friend, Mr. Hobbs, and he went to see him at the store soon after breakfast, in great anxiety of mind.

He found him reading the morning paper, and he approached him with a grave demeanour. He really felt it would be a great shock to Mr. Hobbs to hear what had befallen him, and on his way to the store he had been thinking how it would be best to break the news.

"Hello!" said Mr. Hobbs. "Mornin'!"

"Good-morning," said Cedric.

He did not climb up on the high stool as usual, but sat down on a biscuit-box and clasped his knee, and was so silent for a few moments that Mr. Hobbs finally looked up inquiringly over the top of his newspaper.

"Hello!" he said again.

Cedric gathered all his strength of mind together.

"Mr. Hobbs," he said, "do you remember what we were talking about yesterday morning?"

"Well," replied Mr. Hobbs,—"seems to me it was England."

"Yes," said Cedric; "but just when Mary came for me, you know?"

Mr. Hobbs rubbed the back of his head.

"We was mentioning Queen Victoria and the aristocracy."

"Yes," said Cedric, rather hesitatingly, "and—and earls; don't you know?"

"Why, yes," returned Mr. Hobbs; "that's so!"

"You said," proceeded Cedric, "that you wouldn't have them sitting 'round on your biscuit barrels."

"So I did!" returned Mr. Hobbs, stoutly.

"Mr. Hobbs," said Cedric, "one is sitting on this box now!"

Mr. Hobbs almost jumped out of his chair.

"What!" he exclaimed.

"Yes," Cedric announced, with due modesty; "I am one—or I am going to be. I shan't deceive you."

Mr. Hobbs looked agitated. He rose up suddenly and went to look at the thermometer.

"The mercury's got into your head!" he exclaimed, turning back to examine his young friend's countenance. "It is a hot day! How do you feel?"

He put his big hand on the little boy's hair.

"Thank you," said Ceddie; "I'm all right. There is nothing the matter with my head. I'm sorry to say it's true, Mr. Hobbs. That was what Mary came to take me home for. Mr. Havisham was telling my mamma, and he is a lawyer."

Mr. Hobbs sank into his chair and mopped his forehead with his handkerchief.

"One of us has got a sunstroke!" he exclaimed.

"No," returned Cedric, "we have not. Mr. Havisham came all the way from England to tell us about it. My grandpapa sent him."

Mr. Hobbs stared wildly at the innocent, serious little face before him.

"Who is your grandfather?" he asked.

Cedric put his hand in his pocket and carefully drew out a piece of paper, on which something was written in his own round, irregular hand.

"I couldn't easily remember it, so I wrote it down on this," he said. And he read aloud slowly: "'John Arthur Molyneux Errol, Earl of Dorincourt.' That is his name, and he lives in a castle—in two or three castles, I think. And my papa, who died, was his youngest son; and I shouldn't have been a lord or an earl if my papa hadn't died; and my papa wouldn't have been an earl if his two brothers hadn't died, and my grandpapa has sent for me to come to England."

Mr. Hobbs seemed to grow hotter and hotter. He mopped his forehead and breathed hard. He began to see that something very remarkable had happened.

"Wha—what did you say your name was?" Mr. Hobbs inquired.

"It's Cedric Errol, Lord Fauntleroy," answered Cedric. "That was what Mr. Havisham called me."

"Well," said Mr. Hobbs, "I'll be—jiggered!"

This was an exclamation he always used when he was very much astonished or excited. He could think of nothing else to say just at that puzzling moment.

Cedric looked at Mr. Hobbs wistfully.

"England is a long way off, isn't it?" he asked.

"It's across the Atlantic Ocean," Mr. Hobbs answered.

"That's the worst of it," said Cedric. "Perhaps I shall not see you again for a long time. I don't like to think of that, Mr. Hobbs."

"The best of friends must part," said Mr. Hobbs.

"Well," said Cedric, "we have been friends for a great many years, haven't we?"

"Ever since you was born," Mr. Hobbs answered.

"Ah," remarked Cedric, with a sigh, "I never thought I should have to be an earl then!"

"You think," said Mr. Hobbs, "there's no getting out of it?"

"I'm afraid not," answered Cedric. "My mamma says that my papa would wish me to do it. But if I have to be an earl, I can try to be a good one. I'm not going to be a tyrant."

His conversation with Mr. Hobbs was a long and serious one. Once having got over the first shock, Mr. Hobbs endeavoured to resign himself to the situation, and before the interview was at an end he had asked a great many questions. As Cedric could answer but few of them, he endeavoured to answer them himself, and explained many things in a way which would probably have astonished Mr. Havisham, could that gentleman have heard it.

But then there were many things which astonished Mr. Havisham. He had known all about the old Earl's disappointment in his elder sons and all about his fierce rage at Captain Cedric's American marriage, and he knew how he still hated the gentle little widow and would not speak of her except with bitter and cruel words. He insisted that she was only a common American girl, who had entrapped his son into marrying her because she knew he was an earl's son. The old lawyer himself had more than half believed this was all true. When he had been driven into the cheap street, and his coupé had stopped before the cheap small house, he had felt actually shocked.

When Mary handed him into the small parlour he looked around it critically. It was plainly furnished but it had a home-like look; the few adornments on the walls were in good taste, and about the room were many pretty things which a woman's hand might have made.

The lawyer's experience taught him to read people's characters very shrewdly, and as soon as he saw Cedric's mother he knew that the old Earl had made a great mistake in thinking her a vulgar, mercenary woman.

When he first told Mrs. Errol what he had come for, she turned very pale.

"Oh!" she said; "will he have to be taken away from me? We love each other so much! He is such a happiness to me! He is all I have." And her sweet young voice trembled, and the tears rushed into her eyes. "You do not know what he has been to me!" she said.

The lawyer cleared his throat.

"I am obliged to tell you," he said, "that the Earl of Dorincourt is not—is not very friendly toward you. He is an old man, and his prejudices are very strong. He has always especially disliked America and Americans, and was very much enraged by his son's marriage. I am sorry to be the bearer of so unpleasant a communication, but he is very fixed in his determination not to see you. His plan is that Lord Fauntleroy shall be educated under his own supervision; that he shall live with him. The Earl is attached to Dorincourt Castle, and spends a great deal of time there. Lord Fauntleroy will, therefore, be likely to live chiefly at Dorincourt. The Earl offers to you as a home, Court Lodge, which is situated pleasantly, and is not very far from the castle. He also offers you a suitable income. Lord Fauntleroy will be permitted to visit you; the only stipulation is, that you shall not visit him. You see you will not be really separated from your son."

He felt a little uneasy lest she should begin to cry or make a scene.

But she did not. She went to the window and stood with her face turned away for a few moments.

"Captain Errol was very fond of Dorincourt," she said at last. "He loved England, and everything English. It was always a grief to him that he was parted from his home. I know he would wish, that his son should know the beautiful old places, and be brought up in such a way as would be suitable to his future position."

Then she came back to the table and stood looking up at Mr. Havisham very gently.

"My husband would wish it," she said. "It will be best for my little boy. I know—I am sure the Earl would not be so unkind as to try to teach him not to love me; and I know—even if he tried—that my little boy is too much like his father to be harmed. I hope, that his grandfather will love Ceddie. The little boy has a very affectionate nature; and he has always been loved."

x

Mr. Havisham cleared his throat again. He could not quite imagine the gouty, fiery-tempered old Earl loving any one very much; but he knew that if Ceddie were at all a credit to his name, his grandfather would be proud of him.

"Lord Fauntleroy will be comfortable, I am sure," he replied. "It was with a view to his happiness that the Earl desired that you should be near enough to him to see him frequently."

When the door opened and the child came into the room, he recognised in an instant that here was one of the finest and handsomest little fellows he had ever seen. His beauty was something unusual. He had a strong, lithe, graceful little body and a manly little face; he was so like his father that it was really startling; he had his father's golden hair and his mother's brown eyes. They were innocently fearless eyes; he looked as if he had never feared or doubted anything in his life.

"He is the best-bred-looking and handsomest little fellow I ever saw," was what Mr. Havisham thought. What he said aloud was simply, "And so this is little Lord Fauntleroy."

Cedric did not know he was being observed, and he only behaved himself in his ordinary manner. He shook hands with Mr. Havisham in his friendly way when they were introduced to each other, and he answered all his questions with the unhesitating readiness with which he answered Mr. Hobbs.

The next time Mr. Havisham met him, he had quite a long conversation with him—a conversation which made him smile, and rub his chin with his bony hand several times.

Mrs. Errol had been called out of the parlour, and the lawyer and Cedric were left together.

Mr. Havisham sat in an arm-chair on one side of the open window; on the other side was another still larger chair, and Cedric sat in that and looked at Mr. Havisham. There was a short silence after Mrs. Errol went out, and Cedric seemed to be studying Mr. Havisham, and Mr. Havisham was certainly studying Cedric. He could not make up his mind as to what an elderly gentleman should say to a little boy.

But Cedric relieved him by suddenly beginning the conversation himself.

"Do you know," he said, "I don't know what an earl is?"

"Don't you?" said Mr. Havisham.

"No," replied Ceddie. "And I think when a boy is going to be one, he ought to know. Don't you?"

"Well—yes," answered Mr. Havisham, "An earl is—is a very important person."

"So is a president!" put in Ceddie.

"An earl," Mr. Havisham went on, "is frequently of very ancient lineage——"

"What's that?" asked Ceddie.

"Of very old family—extremely old."

"Ah!" said Cedric, thrusting his hands deeper into his pockets. "I suppose that is the way with the apple-woman near the park. I dare say she is of ancient lin-lenage. She is so old it would surprise you how she can stand up."

Mr. Havisham felt rather at a loss as he looked at his companion's innocent, serious little face.

"I am afraid you did not quite understand me," he explained. "When I said 'ancient lineage' I did not mean old age; I meant that the name of such a family has been known in the world a long time; perhaps for hundreds of years persons bearing that name have been known and spoken of in the history of their country."

"Like George Washington," said Ceddie. "I've heard of him ever since I was born, and he was known about long before that. Mr. Hobbs says he will never be forgotten. That's because of the Declaration of Independence, you know, and the Fourth of July. You see, he was a very brave man."

"The first Earl of Dorincourt," said Mr. Havisham solemnly, "was created an earl four hundred years ago."

"Well, well!" said Ceddie. "That was a long time ago! Did you tell Dearest that? It would int'rust her very much. She always likes to hear cur'us things. What else does an earl do besides being created?"

"A great many of them have helped to govern England. Some of them have been brave men and have fought in great battles in the old days."

"I should like to do that myself," said Cedric. "My papa was a soldier, and he was a very brave man—as brave as George Washington. Perhaps that was because he would have been an earl if he hadn't died. I am glad earls are brave. That's a great 'vantage—to be a brave man."

"There is another advantage in being an earl, sometimes," said Mr. Havisham slowly. "Some earls have a great deal of money."

He was curious because he wondered if his young friend knew what the power of money was.

"That's a good thing to have," said Ceddie innocently. "I wish I had a great deal of money."

"Do you?" said Mr. Havisham. "And why?"

"Well," explained Cedric, "there are so many things a person can do with money. You see there's the apple-woman. If I were very rich I should buy her a little tent to put her stall in, and a little stove, and then I should give her a dollar every morning it rained, so that she could afford to stay at home."

"Ahem!" said Mr. Havisham. "And what else would you do if you were rich?"

"Oh! I'd do a great many things. Of course I should buy Dearest all sorts of beautiful things, needle-books and fans and gold thimbles and rings, and an encyclopedia, and a carriage, so that she needn't have to wait for the street-cars. And then Dick——"

"Who is Dick?" asked Mr. Havisham.

"Dick is a boot-black," said his young lordship, quite warming up in his interest in plans so exciting. "He is one of the nicest boot-blacks you ever knew. He stands at the corner of a street down town. I've known him for years. Once when I was very little, I was walking out with Dearest and she bought me a beautiful ball that bounced, and I was carrying it, and it bounced into the middle of the street where the carriages and horses were, and I was so disappointed, I began to cry—I was very little. Dick ran in between the horses and caught the ball for me and wiped it off with his coat and gave it to me and said; 'It's all right, young un.' So Dearest admired him very much, and so did I, and ever since then, when we go down town, we talk to him."

"And what would you like to do for him?" inquired the lawyer, rubbing his chin and smiling a queer smile.

"Well," said Lord Fauntleroy, settling himself in his chair with a business air; "I'd buy Jake out."

"And who is Jake?" Mr. Havisham asked.

"He's Dick's partner, and he is the worst partner a fellow could have! Dick says so. He isn't a credit to the business, and he isn't square. He cheats, and that makes Dick mad. So if I were rich, I'd buy Jake out and I'd get Dick some new clothes and new brushes, and start him out fair."

"What would you get for yourself, if you were rich?" asked Mr. Havisham.

"Lots of things!" answered Lord Fauntleroy briskly: "but first I'd give Mary some money for Bridget—that's her sister, with twelve children, and a husband out of work. And I think Mr. Hobbs would like a gold watch and chain to remember me by, and a meerschaum pipe."

The door opened and Mrs. Errol came in.

"I am sorry to have been obliged to leave you so long," she said to Mr. Havisham; "but a poor woman, who is in great trouble, came to see me."

"This young gentleman," said Mr. Havisham, "has been telling me about some of his friends, and what he would do for them if he were rich."

"Bridget is one of his friends," said Mrs. Errol; "and it is Bridget to whom I have been talking in the kitchen. She is in great trouble now because her husband has rheumatic fever."

Cedric slipped down out of his big chair.

"I think I'll go and see her," he said, "and ask her how he is. He's a nice man when he is well, he once made me a sword out of wood."

He ran out of the room, and Mr. Havisham rose from his chair. He seemed to have something in his mind which he wished to speak of. He hesitated a moment, and then said, looking down at Mrs. Errol:

"Before I left Dorincourt Castle I had an interview with the Earl, in which he gave me some instructions. He said that I must let his lordship know that the change in his life would bring him money and the pleasures children enjoy; if he expressed any wishes I was to gratify them, and to tell him that his grandfather had given him what he wished. I am aware that the Earl did not expect anything quite like this; but if it would give Lord Fauntleroy pleasure to assist this poor woman, I should feel that the Earl would be displeased if he were not gratified."

"Oh!" Mrs. Errol said, "that was very kind of the Earl; Cedric will be so glad! He has always been fond of Bridget and Michael. They are quite deserving."

Mr. Havisham put his thin hand in his breast pocket and drew forth a large pocket-book. There was a queer look in his keen face. The truth was, he was wondering what the Earl of Dorincourt would say when he was told what was the first wish of his grandson that had been granted.

"I do not know that you have realised," he said, "that the Earl of Dorincourt is an exceedingly rich man. I think it would please him to know that Lord Fauntleroy had been indulged in any fancy. If you will call him back and allow me, I shall give him five pounds for these people."

"That would be twenty-five dollars!" exclaimed Mrs. Errol. "It will seem like wealth to them. I can scarcely believe that it is true."

"It is quite true," said Mr. Havisham, with his dry smile. "A great change has taken place in your son's life, a great deal of power will lie in his hands."

"Oh!" cried his mother. "And he is such a little boy—a very little boy. How can I teach him to use it well? It makes me half afraid. My pretty little Ceddie!"

The lawyer slightly cleared his throat. It touched his worldly, hard old heart to see the tender, timid look in her brown eyes.

"I think, madam," he said, "that if I may judge from my interview with Lord Fauntleroy this morning, the next Earl of Dorincourt will think for others as well as for his noble self. He is only a child yet, but I think he may be trusted."

Then his mother went for Cedric and brought him back into the parlour.

His little face looked quite anxious when he came in. He was very sorry for Bridget.

"Dearest said you wanted me," he said to Mr. Havisham. "I've been talking to Bridget."

Mr. Havisham looked down at him a moment. He felt a little awkward and undecided. As Cedric's mother had said, he was a very little boy.

"The Earl of Dorincourt——" he began, and then he glanced involuntarily at Mrs. Errol.

Little Lord Fauntleroy's mother suddenly kneeled down by him and put both her tender arms around his childish body.

"Ceddie," she said, "the Earl is your grandpapa, your own papa's father. He is very, very kind, and he loves you and wishes you to love him, because the sons who were his little boys are dead. He wishes you to be happy and to make other people happy. He is very rich, and he wishes you to have everything you would like to have. He told Mr. Havisham so, and gave him a great deal of money for you. You can give some to Bridget now, enough to pay her rent and buy Michael everything. Isn't that fine, Ceddie? Isn't he good?" And she kissed the child on his round cheek, where the bright colour suddenly flashed up in his excited amazement.

He looked from his mother to Mr. Havisham.

"Can I have it now?" he cried. "Can I give it to her this minute? She's just going."

Mr. Havisham handed him the money. It was in fresh clean greenbacks and made a neat roll.

Ceddie flew out of the room.

"Bridget!" they heard him shout, as he tore into the kitchen. "Bridget, wait a minute! Here's some money. It's for you, and you can pay the rent. My grandpapa gave it to me. It's for you and Michael!"

"Oh, Master Ceddie!" cried Bridget, in an awestricken voice. "It's twenty-foive dollars is here. Where's the mistress?"

"I think I shall have to go and explain it to her," Mrs. Errol said.

So she, too, went out of the room, and Mr. Havisham was left alone for a while. He went to the window and stood looking out into the street reflectively. He was thinking of the old Earl of Dorincourt, sitting in his great, splendid, gloomy library at the castle, gouty and lonely, surrounded by grandeur and luxury, but not really loved by any one, because in all his long life he had never really loved any one but himself. He could fill his castle with guests if he chose, but he knew that in secret the people who would accept his invitations were afraid of his frowning old face and sarcastic, biting speeches.

Mr. Havisham knew his hard, fierce ways by heart, and he was thinking of him as he looked out of the window into the quiet, narrow street. And there rose in his mind, in sharp contrast, the picture of the cheery, handsome little fellow sitting in the big chair and telling his story of his friends, Dick and the apple-woman, in his generous, innocent, honest way. And he thought of the immense income, the beautiful, majestic estates, the wealth, and power for good or evil, which in the course of time would lie in the small, chubby hands little Lord Fauntleroy thrust so deep into his pockets.

"It will make a great difference," he said to himself. "It will make a great difference."

Cedric and his mother came back soon after. Cedric was in high spirits. He was glowing with enjoyment of Bridget's relief and rapture.

"She cried!" he said. "She said she was crying for joy. I never saw any one cry for joy before. My grandpapa must be a very good man. I didn't know he was so good a man. It's more—more agreeable to be an earl than I thought it was. I'm almost glad—I'm almost quite glad I'm going to be one."

CHAPTER III.

LEAVING HOME.

Cedric's good opinion of the advantages of being an earl increased greatly during the next week. It seemed almost impossible for him to realise that there was scarcely anything he might wish to do which he could not do easily; in fact I think it may be said that he did not fully realise it at all. But at least he understood, after a few conversations with Mr. Havisham, that he could gratify all his nearest wishes, and he proceeded to gratify them with a simplicity and delight which caused Mr. Havisham much diversion. In the week before they sailed for England, he did many curious things. The lawyer long after remembered the morning they went down together to pay a visit to Dick, and the afternoon they so amazed the apple-woman of ancient lineage by stopping before her stall and telling her she was to have a tent, and a stove, and a shawl, and a sum of money which seemed to her quite wonderful.

"For I have to go to England and be a lord," explained Cedric, sweet-temperedly.

"She's a very good apple-woman," he said to Mr. Havisham as they walked away, leaving the proprietress of the stall almost gasping for breath, and not at all believing in her great fortune. "Once, when I fell down and cut my knee, she gave me an apple for nothing. I've always remembered her for it. You know you always remember people who are kind to you."

It had never occurred to his honest, simple, little mind that there were people who could forget kindnesses.

The interview with Dick was quite exciting. Dick had just been having a great deal of trouble with Jake, and was in low spirits when they saw him. His amazement when Cedric calmly announced that they had come to give him what seemed a very great thing to him, and would set all his troubles right, almost struck him dumb. Lord Fauntleroy's manner of announcing the object of his visit was very simple and unceremonious and the end of the matter was that Dick bought Jake out, and found himself the possessor of the business, and some new brushes and a most astonishing sign and outfit. He could not believe in his good luck any more easily than the apple-woman of ancient lineage could believe in hers. He scarcely seemed to realise anything until Cedric put out his hand to shake hands with him before going away.

"Well, good-bye," he said; and though he tried to speak steadily, there was a little tremble in his voice and he winked his big brown eyes. "And I hope trade'll be good. I'm sorry I'm going away to leave you, but I wish you'd write to me, because we were always good friends. And here's where you must send your letter." And he gave him a slip of paper. "And my name isn't Cedric Errol any more; it's Lord Fauntleroy and—and good-bye, Dick."

Dick winked his eyes also, and yet they looked rather moist about the lashes.

"I wish ye wasn't goin' away," he said in a husky voice. Then he winked his eyes again. Then he looked at Mr. Havisham and touched his cap. "Thanky, sir, for bringin' him down here an' fur wot ye've done."

Until the day of his departure, his lordship spent as much time as possible with Mr. Hobbs in the store. Gloom had settled upon Mr. Hobbs; he was much depressed in spirits. When his young friend brought to him in triumph the parting gift of a gold watch and chain, Mr. Hobbs found it difficult to acknowledge it properly. He laid the case on his stout knee, and blew his nose violently several times.

"There's something written on it," said Cedric,—"inside the case. I told the man myself what to say. 'From his oldest friend, Lord Fauntleroy, to Mr. Hobbs. When this you see, remember me.' I don't want you to forget me."

Mr. Hobbs blew his nose very loudly again.

"I shan't forget you," he said, speaking a trifle huskily, as Dick had spoken; "nor don't you go and forget me when you get among the British aristocracy."

"I shouldn't forget you, whoever I was among," answered his lordship. "I've spent my happiest hours with you; at least, some of my happiest hours. I hope you'll come to see me some time."

At last all the preparations were complete; the day came when the trunks were taken to the steamer, and the hour arrived when the carriage stood at the door. Then a curious feeling of loneliness came upon the little boy. His mamma had been shut up in her room for some time; when she came down the stairs, her eyes looked large and wet, and her sweet mouth was trembling. Cedric went to her, and she bent down to him, and he put his arms around her and they kissed each other. He knew something made them both sorry, though he scarcely knew what it was; but one tender little thought rose to his lips.

"We liked this little house, Dearest, didn't we?" he said. "We always will like it, won't we?"

"Yes—yes," she answered in a low, sweet voice. "Yes, darling."

And then they went into the carriage and Cedric sat very close to her, and as she looked back out of the window, he looked at her and stroked her hand and held it close.

And then, it seemed almost directly, they were on the steamer in the midst of the wildest bustle and confusion; carriages were driving down and leaving passengers; passengers were getting into a state of excitement about baggage which had not arrived and threatened to be too late; big trunks and cases were being bumped down and dragged about; sailors were uncoiling ropes and hurrying to and fro; officers were giving orders; ladies and gentlemen and children and nurses were coming on board—some were laughing and looked gay, some were silent and sad, here and there two or three were crying and touching their eyes with their handkerchiefs. Cedric found something to interest him on every side; he looked at the piles of rope, at the furled sails, at the tall, tall masts which seemed almost to touch the hot blue sky; he began to make plans for conversing with the sailors and gaining some information on the subject of pirates.

It was just at the very last, when he was leaning on the railing of the upper deck and watching the final preparations, that his attention was called to a slight bustle in one of the groups not far from him. Some one was hurriedly forcing his way through this group and coming toward him. It was a boy, with something red in his hand. It was Dick. He came up to Cedric quite breathless.

"I've run all the way," he said. "I've come down to see ye off. Trade's been prime! I bought this for ye out o' what I made yesterday. Ye kin wear it when ye get among the swells. It's a hankercher."

He poured it all forth as if in one sentence. A bell rang and he made a leap away before Cedric had time to speak.

"Good-bye!" he panted. "Wear it when ye get among the swells." And he darted off and was gone.

Cedric held the handkerchief in his hand. It was of bright red silk, ornamented with purple horse-shoes and horses' heads, he leaned forward and waved it.

"Good-bye, Dick!" he shouted, lustily. "Thank you! Good-bye, Dick!"

And the big steamer moved away, and the people cheered again, and Cedric's mother drew the veil over her eyes, and on the shore there was left great confusion; but Dick saw nothing save that bright, childish face and the bright hair that the sun shone on and the breeze lifted, and he heard nothing but the hearty childish voice calling "Good-bye, Dick!" as little Lord Fauntleroy steamed slowly away from the home of his birth to the unknown land of his ancestors.

CHAPTER IV.

IN ENGLAND.

It was during the voyage that Cedric's mother told him that his home was not to be hers; and when he first understood it, his grief was so great that Mr. Havisham saw that the Earl had been wise in making the arrangements that his mother should be quite near him, and see him often; for it was very plain he could not have borne the separation otherwise. But his mother managed the little fellow so sweetly and lovingly, and made him feel that she would be so near him, that, after a while, he ceased to be oppressed by the fear of any real parting.

"My house is not far from the Castle, Ceddie," she repeated each time the subject was referred to—"a very little way from yours, and you can always run in and see me every day, and you will have so many things to tell me! and we shall be so happy together! It is a beautiful place. Your papa has often told me about it. He loved it very much; and you will love it too."

"I should love it better if you were there," his small lordship said, with a heavy little sigh.

He could not but feel puzzled by so strange a state of affairs, which could put his "Dearest" in one house and himself in another.

The fact was that Mrs. Errol had thought it better not to tell him why this plan had been made.

"I should prefer he should not be told," she said to Mr. Havisham. "He would not really understand; he would only be shocked and hurt; and I feel sure that his feeling for the Earl will be a more natural and affectionate one if he does not know that his grandfather dislikes me so bitterly. It would make a barrier between them, even though Ceddie is such a child."

So Cedric only knew that there was some mysterious reason for the arrangement, some reason which he was not old enough to understand, but which would be explained when he was older. He was puzzled; but after many talks with his mother, in which she placed before him the bright side of the picture, the dark side of it gradually began to fade out, though now and then Mr. Havisham saw him sitting in some queer little old-fashioned attitude, watching the sea, with a very grave face, and more than once he heard an unchildish sigh rise to his lips.

The people who had been sea-sick had no sooner recovered from their sea-sickness, and come on deck to recline in their steamer-chairs and enjoy themselves, than every one seemed to know the romantic story of Little Lord Fauntleroy, and every one took an interest in the little fellow, who ran about the ship or walked with his mother or the tall, thin old lawyer, or talked to the sailors. Every one liked him, he made friends everywhere. He was ever ready to make friends. When the gentlemen walked up and down the deck, and let him walk with them, he stepped out with a manly, sturdy little tramp, and answered all their jokes with much gay enjoyment; when the ladies talked to him, there was always laughter in the group of which he was the centre; when he played with the children, there was always magnificent fun on hand. Among the sailors he had the heartiest friends; he heard miraculous stories about pirates and shipwrecks and desert islands; he learned to splice ropes and rig toy ships, and gained an amount of information concerning "tops'les" and "mains'les," quite surprising. His conversation had, indeed, quite a nautical flavour at times.

It was eleven days after he had said good-bye to his friend Dick before he reached Liverpool; and it was on the night of the twelfth day that the carriage, in which he and his mother and Mr. Havisham had driven from the station, stopped before the gates of Court Lodge.

Mary had come with them to attend her mistress, and she had reached the house before them. When Cedric jumped out of the carriage Mary stood in the doorway.

Lord Fauntleroy sprang at her with a gay little shout.

"Did you get here, Mary?" he said. "Here's Mary, Dearest."

"I am glad you are here, Mary," Mrs. Errol said to her in a low voice. "It is such a comfort to me to see you. It takes the strangeness away." And she held out her little hand, which Mary squeezed encouragingly.

The English servants looked with curiosity at both the boy and his mother. They had heard all sorts of rumours about them both; they knew why Mrs. Errol was to live at the lodge and her little boy at the Castle; but they did not know what sort of a little lord had come among them; they did not quite understand the character of the next Earl of Dorincourt.

He pulled off his overcoat quite as if he were used to doing things for himself, and began to look about him. He looked about the broad hall, at the pictures and stags' antlers and curious things that ornamented it. They seemed curious to him because he had never seen such things before in a private house.

"Dearest," he said, "this is a very pretty house, isn't it? I am glad you are going to live here. It's quite a large house."

It was quite a large house compared to the one in the shabby New York street, and it was very pretty and cheerful.

Mary led them into a big bright room; its ceiling was low, and the furniture was heavy and beautifully carved. There was a great tiger-skin before the fire, and an arm-chair on each side of it. A stately white cat had responded to Lord Fauntleroy's stroking and followed him down stairs, and when he threw himself down upon the rug, she curled herself up grandly beside him as if she intended to make friends. Cedric was so pleased that he put his head down by hers, and lay stroking her, not noticing what his mother and Mr. Havisham were saying.

They were, indeed, speaking in a rather low tone. Mrs. Errol looked a little pale and agitated.

"He need not go to-night?" she said. "He will stay with me to-night?"

"Yes," answered Mr. Havisham in the same low tone; "it will not be necessary for him to go to-night. I myself will go to the Castle as soon as we have dined, and inform the Earl of our arrival."

Mrs. Errol smiled faintly.

"His lordship does not know all that he is taking from me," she said rather sadly. Then she looked at the lawyer. "Will you tell him, if you please," she said, "that I should rather not have the income he proposed to settle upon me. I am obliged to accept the house, and I thank him for it, because it makes it possible for me to be near my child; but I have a little money of my own and I should rather not take the other. As he dislikes me so much, I should feel a little as if I were selling Cedric to him. I am giving him up only because I love him enough to forget myself for his good, and because his father would wish it to be so."

Mr. Havisham rubbed his chin.

"This is very strange," he said. "He will be very angry. He won't understand it, but I will deliver your message."

And then the dinner was brought in and they sat down together, the big cat taking a seat on a chair near Cedric's and purring majestically throughout the meal.

When, later in the evening, Mr. Havisham presented himself at the Castle, he was taken at once to the Earl. He found him sitting by the fire in a luxurious easy-chair, his foot on a gout-stool. He looked at the lawyer sharply from under his shaggy eyebrows.

"Well," he said; "well, Havisham, come back, have you? What's the news?"

"Lord Fauntleroy and his mother are at Court Lodge," replied Mr. Havisham. "They bore the voyage very well and are in excellent health."

The Earl made a half-impatient sound and moved his hand restlessly.

"Glad to hear it," he said brusquely. "So far, so good. Make yourself comfortable. Have a glass of wine and settle down. What else?"

"His lordship remains with his mother to-night. To-morrow I will bring him to the Castle."

The Earl's elbow was resting on the arm of his chair; he put his hand up and shielded his eyes with it.

"Well?" he said; "go on. What kind of a lad is he? I don't care about the mother; what sort of a lad is he? Healthy and well grown?"

"Apparently very healthy, and quite well grown," replied the lawyer.

"Straight-limbed and well enough to look at?" demanded the Earl.

A very slight smile touched Mr. Havisham's thin lips.

"Rather a handsome boy, I think, my lord, as boys go," he said, "though I am scarcely a judge, perhaps."

There was a silence of a few moments. It was Mr. Havisham who broke it.

“I have a message to deliver from Mrs. Errol,” he remarked.

“I don’t want any of her messages!” growled his lordship; “the less I hear of her the better.”

“This is a rather important one,” explained the lawyer. “She prefers not to accept the income you proposed to settle on her.”

The Earl started visibly.

“What’s that?” he cried out. “What’s that?”

Mr. Havisham repeated his words.

“She says it is not necessary, and that as the relations between you are not friendly——”

“Not friendly!” ejaculated my lord savagely; “I should say they were not friendly! I hate to think of her! A mercenary American! I don’t wish to see her!”

“My lord,” said Mr. Havisham, “you can scarcely call her mercenary. She has asked for nothing. She does not accept the money you offer her.”

“All done for effect!” snapped his noble lordship. “She thinks I shall admire her spirit. I don’t admire it! It’s only American independence! I won’t have her living like a beggar at my park gates. She shall have the money, whether she likes it or not!”

“She won’t spend it,” said Mr. Havisham.

“I don’t care whether she spends it or not!” blustered my lord. “She shall have it sent to her. She wants to give the boy a bad opinion of me! I suppose she has poisoned his mind against me already!”

"No," said Mr. Havisham. "I have another message, which will prove to you that she has not done that."

"I don't want to hear it!" panted the Earl, out of breath with anger and excitement and gout.

But Mr. Havisham delivered it.

"She asks you not to let Lord Fauntleroy hear anything which would lead him to understand that you separate him from her because of your prejudice against her. He is very fond of her, and she is convinced that it would cause a barrier to exist between you. She has told him that he is too young to understand the reason, but shall hear it when he is older. She wishes that there should be no shadow on your first meeting."

The Earl sank back into his chair. His deep-set fierce old eyes gleamed under his beetling brows.

"Come, now!" he said, still breathlessly. "Come, now! You don't mean the mother hasn't told him?"

"Not one word, my lord," replied the lawyer coolly. "That I can assure you. The child is prepared to believe you the most amiable and affectionate of grandparents. And as I carried out your commands in every detail, while in New York, he certainly regards you as a wonder of generosity."

"He does, eh?" said the Earl.

"I give you my word of honour," said Mr. Havisham, "that Lord Fauntleroy's impressions of you will depend entirely upon yourself. And if you will pardon the liberty I take in making the suggestion, I think you will succeed better with him if you take the precaution not to speak slightingly of his mother."

"Pooh, pooh!" said the Earl. "The youngster's only seven years old!"

"He has spent those seven years at his mother's side," returned Mr. Havisham; "and she has all his affection."

CHAPTER V.

AT THE CASTLE.

It was late in the afternoon when the carriage containing little Lord Fauntleroy and Mr. Havisham drove up the long avenue which led to the castle. The Earl had given orders that his grandson should arrive in time to dine with him, and for some reason best known to himself, he had also ordered that the child should be sent alone into the room in which he intended to receive him. As the carriage rolled up the avenue, Lord Fauntleroy sat leaning comfortably against the luxurious cushions, and regarded the prospect with great interest. He was, in fact, interested in everything he saw. He had been interested in the carriage, with its large, splendid horses and their glittering harness; he had been interested in the tall coachman and footman, with their resplendent livery; and he had been especially interested in the coronet on the panels, and had struck up an acquaintance with the footman for the purpose of inquiring what it meant.

The carriage rolled on and on between the great, beautiful trees which grew on each side of the avenue and stretched their broad swaying branches in an arch across it. Cedric had never seen such trees, they were so grand and stately, and their branches grew so low down on their huge trunks. He did not then know that Dorincourt Castle was one of the most beautiful in all England; that its park was one of the broadest and finest, and its trees and avenue almost without rivals. But he did know that it was all very beautiful. Now and then they passed places where tall ferns grew in masses, and again and again the ground was azure with the bluebells swaying in the soft breeze. Several times he started up with a laugh of delight as a rabbit leaped up from under the greenery and scudded away with a twinkle of short white tail behind it. Once a covey of partridges rose with a sudden whir and flew away, and then he shouted and clapped his hands.

"It's a beautiful place, isn't it?" he said to Mr. Havisham. "I never saw such a beautiful place. It's prettier even than Central Park."

He was rather puzzled by the length of time they were on their way.

"How far is it?" he said, at length, "from the gate to the front door?"

"It is between three and four miles," answered the lawyer.

It was not long after this that they saw the castle. It rose up before them stately and beautiful and grey, the last rays of the sun casting dazzling lights on its many windows. It had turrets and battlements and towers; a great deal of ivy grew upon its walls; all the broad open space about it was laid out in terraces and lawns and beds of brilliant flowers.

"It's the most beautiful place I ever saw!" said Cedric, his round face flushing with pleasure. "It reminds any one of a king's palace. I saw a picture of one once in a fairy-book."

He saw the great entrance-door thrown open and many servants standing in two lines looking at him. He wondered why they were standing there, and admired their liveries very much. He did not know that they were there to do honour to the little boy to whom all this splendour would one day belong. At the head of the line of servants there stood an elderly woman in a rich plain black silk gown; she had grey hair and wore a cap. As he entered the hall she stood nearer than the rest, and the child thought from the look in her eyes that she was going to speak to him. Mr. Havisham, who held his hand, paused a moment.

"This is Lord Fauntleroy, Mrs. Mellon," he said. "Lord Fauntleroy, this is Mrs. Mellon, who is the housekeeper."

Cedric gave her his hand, his eyes lighting up.

"Was it you who sent the cat?" he said. "I'm much obliged to you, ma'am."

Mrs. Mellon's handsome old face looked very much pleased.

"The cat left two beautiful kittens here," she said; "they shall be sent up to your lordship's nursery."

Mr. Havisham said a few words to her in a low voice.

"In the library, sir," Mrs. Mellon replied. "His lordship is to be taken there alone."

A few minutes later, the very tall footman in livery, who had escorted Cedric to the library door, opened it and announced: "Lord Fauntleroy, my Lord," in quite a majestic tone.

Cedric crossed the threshold into the room. It was a very large and splendid room, with massive carven furniture in it, and shelves upon shelves of books; the furniture was so dark, and the draperies so heavy, the diamond-paned windows were so deep, and it seemed such a distance from one end of it to the other, that, since the sun had gone down, the effect of it all was rather gloomy. For a moment Cedric thought there was nobody in the room, but soon he saw that by the fire burning on the wide hearth there was a large easy-chair, and that in that chair some one was sitting—some one who did not at first turn to look at him.

But he had attracted attention in one quarter at least. On the floor, by the arm-chair, lay a dog, a huge tawny mastiff, with body and limbs almost as big as a lion's; and this great creature rose majestically and slowly, and marched toward the little fellow with a heavy step.

Then the person in the chair spoke. "Dougal," he called, "come back, sir."

But there was no fear in little Lord Fauntleroy's heart. He put his hand on the big dog's collar and they strayed forward together, Dougal sniffing as he went.

And then the Earl looked up. What Cedric saw was a large old man with shaggy white hair and eyebrows, and a nose like an eagle's beak between his deep fierce eyes. What the Earl saw was a graceful childish figure in a black velvet suit, with a lace collar, and with love-locks waving about the handsome, manly little face, whose eyes met his with a look of innocent good-fellowship. There was a sudden glow of triumph and exultation in the fiery old Earl's heart as he saw what a strong beautiful boy this grandson was, and how unhesitatingly he looked up as he stood with his hand on the big dog's neck.

Cedric came quite close to him.

"Are you the Earl?" he said. "I'm your grandson, you know, that Mr. Havisham brought. I'm Lord Fauntleroy."

He held out his hand because he thought it must be the polite and proper thing to do even with earls. "I hope you are very well," he continued, with the utmost friendliness. "I'm very glad to see you."

The Earl shook hands with him, with a curious gleam in his eyes.

"Glad to see me, are you?" he said.

"Yes," answered Lord Fauntleroy, "very."

There was a chair near him, and he sat down on it; it was a high-backed, rather tall chair, and his feet did not touch the floor when he had settled himself in it, but he seemed to be quite comfortable as he sat there and regarded his august relative intently and modestly.

"Any boy would love his grandfather," continued he, "especially one that had been as kind to him as you have been."

Another queer gleam came into the old nobleman's eyes.

"Oh!" he said, "I have been kind to you, have I?"

"Yes," answered Lord Fauntleroy brightly; "I'm ever so much obliged to you about Bridget, and the apple-woman, and Dick!"

"Bridget!" exclaimed the Earl. "Dick! The apple-woman!"

"Yes," explained Cedric; "the ones you gave me all that money for—the money you told Mr. Havisham to give me if I wanted it."

"Ha!" ejaculated his lordship. "That's it, is it? The money you were to spend as you liked. What did you buy with it? I should like to hear something about that."

He drew his shaggy eyebrows together and looked at the child sharply. He was secretly curious to know in what way the lad had indulged himself.

"Oh!" said Lord Fauntleroy, "perhaps you didn't know about Dick, and the apple-woman and Bridget. I forgot you lived such a long way off from them. They were particular friends of mine. And you see Michael had the fever——"

"Who's Michael?" asked the Earl.

"Michael is Bridget's husband, and they were in great trouble. And Bridget used to come to our house and cry. And the evening Mr. Havisham was there, she was in the kitchen crying because they had almost nothing to eat and couldn't pay the rent; and I went in to see her, and Mr. Havisham sent for me and he said you had given him some money for me. And I ran as fast as I could into the kitchen and gave it to Bridget; and that made it all right; and Bridget could scarcely believe her eyes. That's why I'm so obliged to you."

"Oh!" said the Earl in his deep voice, "that was one of the things you did for yourself, was it? What else?"

"Well, there was Dick," Cedric answered. "You'd like Dick, he's so square."

This was an Americanism the Earl was not prepared for.

"What does that mean?" he inquired.

Lord Fauntleroy paused a moment to reflect. He was not very sure himself what it meant.

"I think it means that he wouldn't cheat any one," he exclaimed; "or hit a boy who was under his size, and that he blacks people's boots very well and makes them shine as much as he can. He's a professional boot-black."

"And he's one of your acquaintances, is he?" said the Earl.

"He's an old friend of mine," replied his grandson. "Not quite as old as Mr. Hobbs, but quite old. He gave me a present just before the ship sailed."

He put his hand into his pocket and drew forth a neatly folded red object and opened it with an air of affectionate pride. It was the red silk handkerchief with the large purple horse-shoes and heads on it.

"He gave me this," said his young lordship. "I shall keep it always. You can wear it round your neck or keep it in your pocket. It's a keepsake. I put some poetry in Mr. Hobbs' watch. It was, 'When this you see, remember me.' When this I see, I shall always remember Dick."

The sensation of the Right Honourable the Earl of Dorincourt could scarcely be described.

He could not help seeing that the little boy took him for a friend and treated him as one, without having any doubt of him at all. It was quite plain as the little fellow sat there in his tall chair and talked in his friendly way that it had never occurred to him that this large, fierce-looking old man could be anything but kind to him, and rather pleased to see him there. And it was plain, too, that, in his childish way, he wished to please and interest his grandfather. Cross, and hard-hearted, and worldly as the old Earl was, he could not help feeling a secret and novel pleasure in this very confidence.

So the old man leaned back in his chair, and led his young companion on to telling him still more of himself, and with that odd gleam in his eyes watched the little fellow as he talked. Lord Fauntleroy was quite willing to answer all his questions and chatted on in his genial little way quite composedly. He told him all about Dick, and the apple-woman, and Mr. Hobbs. In the course of the conversation, he reached the Fourth of July and the Revolution, and was just becoming enthusiastic, when dinner was announced.

Cedric left his chair and went to his noble kinsman. He looked down at his gouty foot.

"Would you like me to help you?" he said politely. "You could lean on me, you know. Once when Mr. Hobbs hurt his foot with a potato-barrel rolling on it, he used to lean on me."

The Earl looked his valiant young relative over from head to foot.

"Do you think you could do it?" he asked gruffly.

"I think I could," said Cedric. "I'm strong. I'm seven, you know. You could lean on your stick on one side, and on me on the other."

"Well," said the Earl, "you may try."

Cedric gave him his stick, and began to assist him to rise. Usually the footman did this, and was violently sworn at when his lordship had an extra twinge of gout.

But this evening he did not swear, though his gouty foot gave him more twinges than one. He chose to try an experiment. He got up slowly and put his hand on the small shoulder presented to him with so much courage. Little Lord Fauntleroy made a careful step forward, looking down at the gouty foot.

"Just lean on me," he said, with encouraging good cheer. "I'll walk very slowly."

If the Earl had been supported by the footman he would have rested less on his stick and more on his assistant's arm. And yet it was part of his experiment to let his grandson feel his burden as no light weight. It was quite a heavy weight indeed, and after a few steps his young lordship's face grew quite hot, and his heart beat rather fast, but he braced himself sturdily.

"Don't be afraid of leaning on me," he panted. "I'm all right—if—if it isn't a very long way."

It was not really very far to the dining-room, but it seemed rather a long way to Cedric, before they reached the chair at the head of the table.

When the hand was removed from his shoulder, and the Earl was fairly seated, Cedric took out Dick's handkerchief and wiped his forehead.

"It's a warm night, isn't it?" he said.

"You have been doing some rather hard work," said the Earl.

"Oh, no!" said Lord Fauntleroy, "it wasn't exactly hard, but I got a little warm. A person will get warm in summer time."

And he rubbed his damp curls rather vigorously with the gorgeous handkerchief. His own chair was placed at the other end of the table, opposite his grandfather's. It was a chair with arms, and intended for a much larger individual than himself; indeed, everything he had seen so far—the great rooms, with their high ceilings, the massive furniture, the big footman, the big dog, the Earl himself—were all of proportions calculated to make this little lad feel that he was very small indeed. But that did not trouble him.

Notwithstanding his solitary existence the Earl chose to live in considerable state. He was fond of his dinner, and he dined in a formal style. Cedric looked at him across a glitter of splendid glass and plate, which to his unaccustomed eyes seemed quite dazzling. A stranger looking on might well have smiled at the picture—the great stately room, the big liveried servants, the bright lights, the glittering silver and glass, the fierce-looking old nobleman at the head of the table and the very small boy at the foot. Dinner was usually a very serious matter with the Earl—and it was a very serious matter with the cook, if his lordship was not pleased or had an indifferent appetite. To-day, however, his appetite seemed a trifle better than usual, perhaps because his grandson gave him something to think of. He kept looking at him across the table. He did not say very much himself, but he managed to make the boy talk. He had never imagined that he could be entertained by hearing a child talk, but Lord Fauntleroy at once puzzled and amused him.

Cedric finished his dinner first, and then he leaned back in his chair and took a survey of the room.

"You must be very proud of your house," he said, "it's such a beautiful house. I never saw anything so beautiful; but, of course, as I'm only seven, I haven't seen much."

"And you think I must be proud of it, do you?" said the Earl.

"I should think any one would be proud of it," replied Lord Fauntleroy. "I should be proud of it, if it were my house. Everything about it is beautiful."

Then he paused an instant and looked across the table rather wistfully.

"It's a very big house for just two people to live in, isn't it?" he said.

"It is quite large enough for two," answered the Earl. "Do you find it too large?"

His little lordship hesitated a moment.

"I was only thinking," he said, "that if two people lived in it who were not very good companions, they might feel lonely sometimes."

"Do you think I shall make a good companion?" inquired the Earl.

"Yes," replied Cedric, "I think you will. Mr. Hobbs and I were great friends. He was the best friend I had except Dearest."

The Earl made a quick movement of his bushy eyebrows.

"Who is Dearest?"

"She is my mother," said Lord Fauntleroy, in a rather low, quiet little voice.

Perhaps he was a trifle tired, as his bed-time was nearing, and perhaps the feeling of weariness brought to him a vague sense of loneliness in the remembrance that to-night he was not to sleep at home, watched over by the loving eyes of that "best friend" of his. They had always been "best friends," this boy and his young mother. He could not help thinking of her, and the more he thought of her the less was he inclined to talk, and by the time the dinner was at an end the Earl saw that there was a faint shadow on his face. But Cedric bore himself with excellent courage, and when they went back to the library, though the tall footman walked on one side of his master, the Earl's hand rested on his grandson's shoulder, though not so heavily as before.

When the footman left them alone, Cedric sat down upon the hearth-rug near Dougal. For a few minutes he stroked the dog's ears in silence and looked at the fire.

The Earl watched him. The boy's eyes looked wistful and thoughtful, and once or twice he gave a little sigh. The Earl sat still, and kept his eyes fixed on his grandson.

"Fauntleroy," he said at last, "what are you thinking of?"

Fauntleroy looked up with a manful effort at a smile.

"I was thinking about Dearest," he said; "and—and I think I'd better get up and walk up and down the room."

He rose up, and put his hands in his small pockets, and began to walk to and fro. His eyes were very bright, and his lips were pressed together, but he kept his head up and walked firmly. Dougal moved lazily and looked at him and then stood up. He walked over to the child, and began to follow him uneasily. Fauntleroy drew one hand from his pocket and laid it on the dog's head.

"He's a very nice dog," he said. "He's my friend. He knows how I feel."

"How do you feel?" asked the Earl.

"I never was away from my own house before," said the boy, with a troubled look in his brown eyes. "It makes a person feel a strange feeling when he has to stay all night in another person's castle instead of in his own house. But Dearest is not very far away from me. She told me to remember that—and—and I'm seven—and I can look at the picture she gave me."

He put his hand in his pocket, and brought out a small violet velvet-covered case.

"This is it," he said. "You see, you press this spring and it opens, and she is in there!"

He had come close to the Earl's chair, and, as he drew forth the little case, he leaned against the old man's arm.

"There she is," he said, as the case opened; and he looked up with a smile.

The Earl knitted his brows; he did not wish to see the picture, but he looked at it in spite of himself; and there looked up at him from it such a pretty young face—a face so like the child's at his side—that it quite startled him.

"I suppose you think you are very fond of her?" he said.

"Yes," answered Lord Fauntleroy, in a gentle tone, and with simple directness; "I do think so, and I think it's true. You see Mr. Hobbs was my friend, and Dick and Bridget and Michael they were my friends too; but Dearest—well she is my close friend, and we always tell each other everything."

His young lordship slipped down upon the hearth-rug, and sat there with the picture still in his hand.

The Earl did not speak again. He leaned back in his chair and watched him. A great many strange new thoughts passed through the old nobleman's mind. Dougal had stretched himself out and gone to sleep with his head on his huge paws. There was a long silence.

In about half an hour's time Mr. Havisham was ushered in. The great room was very still when he entered. The Earl was still leaning back in his chair. He moved as Mr. Havisham approached, and held up his hand in a gesture of warning—it seemed as if he had scarcely intended to make the gesture—as if it were almost involuntary. Dougal was still asleep, and close beside the great dog, sleeping also, with his curly head upon his arm, lay little Lord Fauntleroy.

CHAPTER VI.

THE EARL AND HIS GRANDSON.

When Lord Fauntleroy wakened in the morning—he had not wakened at all when he had been carried to bed the night before,—the first sound he was conscious of were the crackling of a wood fire and the murmur of voices.

He moved on his pillow, and turned over, opening his eyes.

There were two women in the room. Everything was bright and cheerful with gay-flowered chintz. There was a fire on the hearth, and the sunshine was streaming in through the ivy-entwined windows. Both women came toward him, and he saw that one of them was Mrs. Mellon, the housekeeper, and the other a comfortable, middle-aged woman, with a face as kind and good-humoured as a face could be.

"Good-morning, my lord," said Mrs. Mellon. "Did you sleep well?"

His lordship rubbed his eyes and smiled.

"Good-morning," he said. "I didn't know I was here."

"You were carried up-stairs when you were asleep," said the housekeeper. "This is your bedroom, and this is Dawson, who is to take care of you."

Fauntleroy sat up in bed and held out his hand to Dawson, as he had held it out to the Earl.

"How do you do, ma'am?" he said. "I'm much obliged to you for coming to take care of me."

"You can call her Dawson, my lord," said the housekeeper with a smile. "She is used to being called Dawson.—She will do anything you ask her to."

"That I will, bless him," said Dawson, in her comforting, good-humoured voice. "He shall dress himself, and I'll stand by, ready to help him if he wants me."

"Thank you," responded Lord Fauntleroy; "it's a little hard sometimes about the buttons, you know, and then I have to ask somebody."

When he went into the adjoining room to take his breakfast and saw what a great room it was, and found there was another adjoining it, which Dawson told him was his also, the feeling that he was very small indeed came over him again so strongly that he confided it to Dawson, as he sat down to the table on which the pretty breakfast service was arranged.

"I am a very little boy," he said rather wistfully, "to live in such a large castle, and have so many big rooms—don't you think so?"

"Oh, come!" said Dawson, "you feel just a little strange at first, that's all; but you'll get over that very soon, and then you'll like it here. It's such a beautiful place, you know."

"It's a very beautiful place, of course," said Fauntleroy, with a little sigh; "but I should like it better if I didn't miss Dearest so. I always had my breakfast with her in the morning, and put the sugar and cream in her tea for her, and handed her the toast. That made it very sociable, of course."

"Oh, well!" answered Dawson, comfortably, "you know you can see her every day, and there's no knowing how much you'll have to tell her. Bless you! wait till you've walked about a bit and seen things—the dogs and the stables with all the horses in them. And, dear me, you haven't looked even into the very next room yet!"

"What is there?" asked Fauntleroy,

"Wait until you've had your breakfast, and then you shall see," said Dawson.

At this he naturally began to grow curious, and he applied himself assiduously to his breakfast.

"Now then," he said, slipping off his seat a few minutes later; "I've had enough. Can I go and look at it?"

Dawson nodded and led the way.

When she opened the door of the room, he stood upon the threshold and looked about him in amazement. He did not speak; he only put his hands in his pockets and stood there looking in.

The room was a large one too, as all the rooms seemed to be, and it appeared to him more beautiful than the rest, only in a different way. The furniture was not so massive and antique as was that in the rooms he had seen down stairs; the draperies and rugs and walls were brighter; there were shelves full of books, and on the tables were numbers of toys—beautiful, ingenious things—such as he had looked at with wonder and delight through the shop windows in New York.

"It looks like a boy's room," he said at last, catching his breath a little. "Who do they belong to?"

"Go and look at them," said Dawson. "They belong to you!"

"To me!" he cried "to me! Why do they belong to me? Who gave them to me?" And he sprang forward with a gay little shout. It seemed almost too much to be believed. "It was Grandpapa!" he said, with his eyes as bright as stars. "I know it was Grandpapa!"

"Yes, it was his lordship," said Dawson.

It was a tremendously exciting morning. There were so many things to be examined, so many experiments to be tried; each novelty was so absorbing that he could scarcely turn from it to look at the next.

The Earl had passed a bad night and had spent the morning in his room; but at noon, after he had lunched, he sent for his grandson.

Fauntleroy answered the summons at once. He came down the broad staircase with a bounding step; the Earl heard him run across the hall, and then the door opened and he came in with red cheeks and sparkling eyes.

"I was waiting for you to send for me," he said. "I was ready a long time ago. I'm ever so much obliged to you for all those things! I'm ever so much obliged to you! I have been playing with them all the morning."

"Oh!" said the Earl, "you like them, do you?"

"I like them so much—well, I couldn't tell you how much!" said Fauntleroy, his face glowing with delight. "There's one that's like base-ball. I tried to teach Dawson, but she couldn't quite understand it just at first. But you know all about it, don't you?"

"I'm afraid I don't," replied the Earl. "It's an American game, isn't it? Is it something like cricket?"

"I never saw cricket," said Fauntleroy; "but Mr. Hobbs took me several times to see base-ball. It's a splendid game. You get so excited! Would you like me to go and get my game and show it to you? Perhaps it would amuse you and make you forget about your foot. Does your foot hurt you very much this morning?"

"More than I enjoy," was the answer.

"Then perhaps you couldn't forget it," said the little fellow, anxiously. "Perhaps it would bother you to be told about the game. Do you think it would amuse you, or do you think it would bother you?"

"Go and get it," said the Earl.

It certainly was a novel entertainment this—making a companion of a child who offered to teach him to play games, but the very novelty of it amused him. There was a smile lurking about the Earl's mouth when Cedric came back with the box containing the game in his arms, and an expression of the most eager interest on his face.

"May I pull that little table over here to your chair?" he asked.

"Ring for Thomas," said the Earl. "He will place it for you."

"Oh, I can do it myself," answered Fauntleroy. "It's not very heavy."

"Very well," replied his grandfather. The lurking smile deepened on the old man's face as he watched the little fellow's preparations; there was such an absorbed interest in them. The small table was dragged forward and placed by his chair, and the game taken from its box and arranged upon it.

"It's very interesting when you once begin," said Fauntleroy. "You see, the black pegs can be your side and the white ones mine. They're men, you know, and once round the field is a home run and counts one—and these are the outs—and here is the first base and that's the second and that's the third and that's the home-base."

He entered into the details of explanation with the greatest animation. He showed all the attitudes of pitcher and catcher and batter in the real game.

When at last the explanations and illustrations were at an end and the game began in good earnest, the Earl still found himself entertained. His young companion was wholly absorbed; he played with all his childish heart; his gay little laughs when he made a good throw, his enthusiasm over a "home run," his impartial delight over his own good luck or his opponent's would have given a flavour to any game.

If, a week before, any one had told the Earl of Dorincourt that on that particular morning he would be forgetting his gout and his bad temper in a child's game, with a curly-headed small boy for a companion, he would without doubt have made himself very unpleasant; and yet he certainly had forgotten himself when the door opened and Thomas announced a visitor.

The visitor in question, who was an elderly gentleman in black, and no less a person than the clergyman of the parish, was so startled by the amazing scene which met his eye, that he almost fell back a pace, and ran some risk of colliding with Thomas.

There, was, in fact, no part of his duty that the Reverend Mr. Mordaunt found so decidedly unpleasant as that part which compelled him to call upon his noble patron at the Castle. His noble patron, indeed, usually made these visits as disagreeable as it lay in his lordly power to make them. He abhorred churches and charities, and flew into violent rages when any of his tenantry took the liberty of being poor and ill and needing assistance. During all the years in which Mr. Mordaunt had been in charge of Dorincourt parish, the rector certainly did not remember having seen his lordship, of his own free will, do any one a kindness, or, under any circumstances whatever, show that he thought of any one but himself.

Judge then of his amazement when, as Thomas opened the library door, his ears were greeted by a delighted ring of childish laughter.

The Earl glanced around, and when he saw who it was, Mr. Mordaunt was still more surprised to see that he looked almost as if he had forgotten for the moment how unpleasant he really could make himself when he tried.

"Ah!" he said in his harsh voice, but giving his hand rather graciously. "Good morning, Mordaunt. I've found a new employment, you see."

He put his other hand on Cedric's shoulder—perhaps deep down in his heart there was a stir of gratified pride that it was such an heir he had to present; there was a spark of something like pleasure in his eyes as he moved the boy slightly forward.

"This is the new Lord Fauntleroy," he said. "Fauntleroy, this is Mr. Mordaunt, the rector of the parish."

Fauntleroy looked up at the gentleman in the clerical garments, and gave him his hand.

"I am very glad to make your acquaintance, sir," he said.

Mr. Mordaunt held the small hand in his a moment as he looked down at the child's face, smiling involuntarily, He liked the little fellow from that instant—as in fact people always did like him.

"I am delighted to make your acquaintance, Lord Fauntleroy," said the rector. "You made a long journey to come to us. A great many people will be glad to know you made it safely."

"It was a long way," answered Fauntleroy; "but Dearest, my mother, was with me and I wasn't lonely. Of course you are never lonely if your mother is with you; and the ship was beautiful."

"Take a chair, Mordaunt," said the Earl. Mr. Mordaunt sat down. He glanced from Fauntleroy to the Earl.

"Your lordship is greatly to be congratulated," he said warmly. But the Earl plainly had no intention of showing his feelings on the subject.

"He is like his father," he said rather gruffly. "Let us hope he'll conduct himself more creditably." And then he added: "Well, what is it this morning, Mordaunt? Who is in trouble now?"

This was not as bad as Mr. Mordaunt had expected, but he hesitated a second before he began.

"It is Higgins," he said; "Higgins of Edge Farm. He has been very unfortunate. He was ill himself last autumn, and his children had scarlet fever. He is in trouble about his rent now. Newick tells him if he doesn't pay it he must leave the place; and of course that would be a very serious matter. His wife is ill, and he came to me yesterday to beg me to see you about it, and ask you for time. He thinks if you would give him time he could catch up again."

"They all think that," said the Earl, looking rather black.

Fauntleroy made a movement forward. He had been standing between his grandfather and the visitor, listening with all his might. He had begun to be interested in Higgins at once. He wondered how many children there were, and if the scarlet fever had hurt them very much. His eyes were wide open and were fixed upon Mr. Mordaunt with intense interest as that gentleman went on with the conversation.

"Higgins is a well-meaning man," said the rector, making an effort to strengthen his plea.

"He is a bad enough tenant," replied his lordship. "And he is always behindhand, Newick tells me."

"He is in great trouble now," said the rector, "He is very fond of his wife and children, and if the farm is taken from him they may literally starve. He cannot give them the nourishing things they need. Two of the children were left very low after the fever, and the doctor orders for them wine and luxuries that Higgins cannot afford."

At this Fauntleroy moved a step nearer.

"That was the way with Michael," he said.

The Earl slightly started. "I forgot you!" he said. "I forgot we had a philanthropist in the room. Who was Michael?" And the gleam of queer amusement came back into the old man's deep-set eyes.

"He was Bridget's husband, who had the fever," answered Fauntleroy; "and he couldn't pay the rent or buy wine and things. And you gave me that money to help him."

The Earl drew his brows together into a curious frown, which somehow was scarcely grim at all. He glanced across at Mr. Mordaunt.

"I don't know what sort of a landed proprietor he will make," he said. "I told Havisham the boy was to have what he wanted—and what he wanted, it seems, was money to give to beggars."

"Oh! but they weren't beggars," said Fauntleroy eagerly. "Michael was a splendid bricklayer! They all worked."

"Oh!" said the Earl, "they were not beggars."

He bent his gaze on the boy for a few seconds in silence. "Come here," he said, at last.

"What would you do in this case?"

It must be confessed that Mr. Mordaunt experienced for the moment a curious sensation. Being a man of great thoughtfulness, and having spent so many years on the estate of Dorincourt, he realised very strongly what power for good or evil would be given in the future to this one small boy standing there, his brown eyes wide open, his hands deep in his pockets; and the thought came to him also that a great deal of power might, perhaps, through the caprice of a proud, self-indulgent old man be given to him now, and that if his young nature were not a simple and generous one, it might be the worst thing that could happen, not only for others, but for himself.

"And what would you do in such a case?" demanded the Earl.

Fauntleroy drew a little nearer, and laid one hand on his knee, with the most confiding air of good comradeship.

"If I were very rich," he said "and not only just a little boy, I should let him stay, and give him the things for his children; but then, I am only a boy." Then, after a second's pause, in which his face brightened visibly, "You can do anything, can't you?" he said.

"Humph!" said my lord, staring at him. "That's your opinion, is it?" And he was not displeased either.

"I mean you can give any one anything," said Fauntleroy. "Who's Newick?"

"He is my agent," answered the Earl, "and some of my tenants are not over-fond of him."

"Are you going to write him a letter now?" inquired Fauntleroy. "Shall I bring you the pen and ink? I can take the game off this table."

It plainly had not for an instant occurred to him that Newick would be allowed to do his worst.

The Earl paused a moment, still looking at him. "Can you write?" he asked.

"Yes," answered Cedric, "but not very well."

"Move the things from the table," commanded my lord, "and bring the pen and ink, and a sheet of paper from my desk."

Mr. Mordaunt's interest began to increase. Fauntleroy did as he was told very deftly. In a few moments, the sheet of paper, the big inkstand, and the pen were ready.

"There!" he said gaily, "now you can write it."

"You are to write it," said the Earl.

"I!" exclaimed Fauntleroy, and a flush overspread bis forehead. "Will it do if I write it? I don't always spell quite right when I haven't a dictionary and nobody tells me."

"It will do," answered the Earl. "Higgins will not complain of the spelling. I'm not the philanthropist; you are. Dip your pen in the ink."

Fauntleroy took up the pen and dipped it in the ink-bottle, then he arranged himself in position, leaning on the table.

"Now," he inquired, "what must I say?"

"You may say, 'Higgins is not to be interfered with, for the present,' and sign it 'Fauntleroy,'" said the Earl.

Fauntleroy dipped his pen in the ink again, and resting his arm, began to write. It was rather a slow and serious process, but he gave his whole soul to it. After a while, however, the manuscript was complete, and he handed it to his grandfather with a smile slightly tinged with anxiety.

"Do you think it will do?" he asked.

The Earl looked at it, and the corners of his mouth twitched a little.

"Yes," he answered; "Higgins will find it entirely satisfactory." And he handed it to Mr. Mordaunt.

What Mr. Mordaunt found written was this:—

"Dear mr. Newik if you pleas mr. higins is not to be inturfeared with for the present and oblige

"Yours rispecferly

"Fauntleroy."

"Mr. Hobbs always signed his letters that way," said Fauntleroy; "and I thought I'd better say 'please.' Is that exactly the right way to spell 'interfered'?"

"It's not exactly the way it is spelled in the dictionary," answered the Earl.

"I was afraid of that," said Fauntleroy. "I ought to have asked. You see, that's the way with words of more than one syllable; you have to look in the dictionary. It's always safest. I'll write it over again."

And write it over again he did, making quite an imposing copy, and taking precautions in the matter of spelling by consulting the Earl himself.

"Spelling is a curious thing," he said. "It's so often different from what you expect it to be. I used to think 'please' was spelled p-l-e-e-s, but it isn't, you know; and you'd think 'dear' was spelled d-e-r-e, if you didn't inquire. Sometimes it almost discourages you."

When Mr. Mordaunt went away, he took the letter with him, and he took something else with him also—namely, a pleasanter feeling and a more hopeful one than he had ever carried home with him down that avenue on any previous visit he had made at Dorincourt Castle.

When he was gone, Fauntleroy, who had accompanied him to the door, went back to his grandfather.

"May I go to Dearest now?" he said. "I think she will be waiting for me."

The Earl was silent a moment.

"There is something in the stable for you to see first," he said. "Ring the bell."

"If you please," said Fauntleroy, with his quick little flush, "I'm very much obliged; but I think I'd better see it to-morrow. She will be expecting me all the time."

"Very well," answered the Earl. "We will order the carriage." Then he added dryly, "It's a pony."

Fauntleroy drew a long breath.

"A pony!" he exclaimed. "Whose pony is it?"

"Yours," replied the Earl.

"Mine?" cried the little fellow. "Mine—like the things up stairs?"

"Yes," said his grandfather. "Would you like to see it? Shall I order it to be brought round?" Fauntleroy's cheeks grew redder and redder.

"I never thought I should have a pony!" he said. "I never thought that! How glad Dearest will be. You give me everything, don't you?"

"Do you wish to see it?" inquired the Earl.

Fauntleroy drew a long breath. "I want to see it," he said. "I want to see it so much I can hardly wait. But I'm afraid there isn't time."

"You must go and see your mother this afternoon?" asked the Earl. "You think you can't put it off?"

"Why," said Fauntleroy, "she has been thinking about me all the morning, and I have been thinking about her!"

"Oh!" said the Earl. "You have, have you? Ring the bell."

As they drove down the avenue, under the arching trees, he was rather silent. But Fauntleroy was not. He talked about the pony. What colour was it? How big was it? What was its name? What did it like to eat best? How old was it? How early in the morning might he get up and see it?

"Dearest will be so glad!" he kept saying. "She will be so much obliged to you for being so kind to me! She knows I always liked ponies so much, but we never thought I should have one."

He leaned back against the cushions and regarded the Earl with rapt interest for a few minutes and in entire silence.

"I think you must be the best person in the world," he burst forth at last. "You are always doing good, aren't you?—and thinking about other people. Dearest says that is the best kind of goodness; not to think about yourself, but to think about other people. That is just the way you are, isn't it?"

His lordship was so dumfounded to find himself presented in such agreeable colours, that he did not know exactly what to say.

Fauntleroy went on, still regarding him with admiring eyes—those great, clear, innocent eyes!

"You make so many people happy," he said. "There's Michael and Bridget and their ten children, and the apple-woman, and Dick, and Mr. Hobbs, and Mr. Higgins and Mrs. Higgins and their children, and Mr. Mordaunt—because of course he was glad—and Dearest and me, about the pony and all the other things. Do you know, I've counted it up on my fingers and in my mind, and it's twenty-seven people you've been kind to. That's a good many—twenty-seven!"

"And I was the person who was kind to them—was I?" said the Earl.

"Why, yes, you know," answered Fauntleroy. "You made them all happy. Do you know," with some delicate hesitation, "that people are sometimes mistaken about earls when they don't know them? Mr. Hobbs was. I am going to write to him, and tell him about it."

"What was Mr. Hobbs's opinion of earls?" asked his lordship.

"Well, you see, the difficulty was," replied his young companion, "that he didn't know any, and he'd only read about them in books. He thought—you mustn't mind it—that they were gory tyrants; and he said he wouldn't have them hanging around his store. But if he'd known you, I'm sure he would have felt quite different. I shall tell him about you."

"What shall you tell him?"

"I shall tell him," said Fauntleroy, glowing with enthusiasm, "that you are the kindest man I ever heard of. And—and I hope when I grow up, I shall be just like you."

"Just like me!" repeated his lordship, looking at the little kindling face.

"Just like you," said Fauntleroy, adding modestly, "if I can. Perhaps I'm not good enough but I'm going to try."

The carriage rolled on down the stately avenue under the beautiful, broad-branched trees, through the spaces of green shade and lanes of golden sunlight. Fauntleroy saw again the lovely places where the ferns grew high and the bluebells swayed in the breeze; he saw the deer, standing or lying in the deep grass, turn their large startled eyes as the carriage passed, and caught glimpses of the brown rabbits as they scurried away. He heard the whirr of the partridges and the calls and songs of the birds, and it all seemed even more beautiful to him than before. All his heart was filled with pleasure and happiness in the beauty that was on every side. But the old Earl saw and heard very different things, though he was apparently looking out too. He saw a long life, in which there had been neither generous deeds nor kind thoughts; he saw years in which a man who had been young and strong and rich and powerful had used his youth and strength and wealth and power only to please himself and kill time as the days and years succeeded each other; he saw this man, when the time had been killed and old age had come, solitary and without real friends in the midst of all his splendid wealth; he saw people who disliked or feared him, and people who would flatter and cringe to him, but no one who really cared whether he lived or died, unless they had something to gain or lose by it.

And the fact was, indeed, that he had never before condescended to reflect upon it at all, and he only did so now because a child had believed him better than he was.

Fauntleroy thought the Earl's foot must be hurting him, his brows knitted themselves together so, as he looked out at the park; and thinking this, the considerate little fellow tried not to disturb him, and enjoyed the trees and the ferns and the deer in silence. But at last, the carriage, having passed the gates and bowled through the green lanes for a short distance, stopped. They had reached Court Lodge; and Fauntleroy was out upon the ground almost before the big footman had time to open the carriage door.

The Earl wakened from his reverie with a start.

"What!" he said. "Are we here?"

"Yes," said Fauntleroy. "Let me give you your stick. Just lean on me when you get out."

"I am not going to get out," replied his lordship brusquely.

"Not—not to see Dearest?" exclaimed Fauntleroy with astonished face.

"'Dearest' will excuse me," said the Earl dryly. "Go to her and tell her that not even a new pony would keep you away."

"She will be disappointed," said Fauntleroy. "She will want to see you very much."

"I am afraid not," was the answer. "The carriage will call for you as we come back.—Tell Jeffries to drive on, Thomas."

Thomas closed the carriage door: and, after a puzzled look, Fauntleroy ran up the drive. The Earl had the opportunity—of seeing a pair of handsome, strong little legs flash over the ground with astonishing rapidity. Evidently their owner had no intention of losing any time. The carriage rolled slowly away, but his lordship did not at once lean back; he still looked out. Through a space in the trees he could see the house door; it was wide open.
The little figure dashed up the steps; another figure—a little figure too, slender and young, in its black gown—ran to meet it. It seemed as if they flew together, as Fauntleroy leaped into his mother's arms, hanging about her neck and covering her sweet young face with kisses.

CHAPTER VII.

AT CHURCH.

On the following Sunday morning, Mr. Mordaunt had a large congregation. Indeed, he could scarcely remember any Sunday on which the church had been so crowded. People appeared upon the scene who seldom did him the honour of coming to hear his sermons. There were even people from Hazelton, which was the next parish. There were hearty, sunburned farmers, stout, comfortable, apple-cheeked wives in their best bonnets and most gorgeous shawls, and half a dozen children or so to each family. The doctor's wife was there, with her four daughters. Mrs. Kimsey and Mr. Kimsey, who kept the druggist's shop, and made pills, and did up powders for everybody within ten miles, sat in their pew; Mrs. Dibble in hers, Miss Smiff, the village dressmaker, and her friend Miss Perkins, the milliner, sat in theirs; the doctor's young man was present, and the druggist's apprentice; in fact, almost every family on the country side was represented, in one way or another.

In the course of the preceding week, many wonderful stories had been told of little Lord Fauntleroy.

The Reverend Mr. Mordaunt had told the story of Higgins at his own dinner table, and the servant who had heard it had told it in the kitchen, and from there it had spread like wildfire.

And on market-day, when Higgins had appeared in town, he had been questioned on every side, and Newick had been questioned too, and in response had shown to two or three people the note signed "Fauntleroy."

And so the farmers' wives had found plenty to talk of over their tea and their shopping, and they had done the subject full justice and made the most of it. And on Sunday they had either walked to church or had been driven in their gigs by their husbands, who were perhaps a trifle curious themselves about the new little lord who was to be in time the owner of the soil.

It was by no means the Earl's habit to attend church, but he chose to appear on this first Sunday—it was his whim to present himself in the huge family pew, with Fauntleroy at his side.

There were many loiterers in the churchyard that morning. There were groups at the gates and in the porch, and there had been much discussion as to whether my lord would really appear or not. When this discussion was at its height, one good woman suddenly uttered an exclamation.

"Eh!" she said; "that must be the mother, pretty young thing."

All who heard turned and looked at the slender figure in black coming up the path. The veil was thrown back from her face and they could see how fair and sweet it was, and how the bright hair curled as softly as a child's under the little widow's cap.

She was not thinking of the people about; she was thinking of Cedric, and of his visits to her, and of his joy over his new pony, on which he had actually ridden to her door the day before, sitting very straight and looking very proud and happy. But soon she could not help being attracted by the fact that she was being looked at and that her arrival had created some sort of sensation. She first noticed it because an old woman in a red cloak made a bobbing curtsy to her, and then another did the same thing and said, "God bless you, my lady!" and one man after another took off his hat as she passed. For a moment she did not understand, and then she realised that it was because she was little Lord Fauntleroy's mother that they did so, and she flushed rather shyly, and smiled and bowed too and said, "Thank you" in a gentle voice to the old woman, who had blessed her. She had scarcely passed through the stone porch into the church before the great event of the day happened. The carriage from the Castle, with its handsome horses and tall liveried servants, bowled round the corner and down the green lane.

"Here they come!" went from one looker-on to another.

And then the carriage drew up, and Thomas stepped down and opened the door, and a little boy, dressed in black velvet, and with a splendid mop of bright waving hair, jumped out.

Every man, woman, and child looked curiously upon him.

"He's the Captain over again!" said those of the on-lookers who remembered his father. "He's the Captain's self, to the life!"

He stood there in the sunlight looking up at the Earl, as Thomas helped that nobleman out, with the most affectionate interest that could be imagined. The instant he could help, he put out his hand and offered his shoulder as if he had been seven feet high. It was plain enough to every one that however it might be with other people, the Earl of Dorincourt struck no terror into the breast of his grandson.

"Just lean on me," they heard him say. "How glad the people are to see you, and how well they all seem to know you!"

"Take off your cap, Fauntleroy," said the Earl. "They are bowing to you."

"To me!" cried Fauntleroy, whipping off his cap in a moment, baring his bright head to the crowd, and turning shining, puzzled eyes on them as he tried to bow to every one at once.

"God bless your lordship!" said the curtsying, red-cloaked old woman who had spoken to his mother; "long life to you!"

"Thank you, ma'am," said Fauntleroy. And then they went into the church, and were looked at there, on their way up the aisle to the square red-cushioned and curtained pew. When Fauntleroy was fairly seated he made two discoveries which pleased him: the first was that, across the church where he could look at her, his mother sat and smiled at him; the second, that at one end of the pew against the wall knelt two quaint figures carven in stone, facing each other as they kneeled on either side of a pillar supporting two stone missals, their hands folded as if in prayer, their dress very antique and strange. On the tablet by them was written something of which he could only read the curious words:

"Here lyethe ye bodye of Gregorye Arthure Fyrst Earle of Dorincourt allsoe of Alisone Hildegarde hys wyfe."

"May I whisper?" inquired his lordship, devoured by curiosity.

"What is it?" said his grandfather.

"Who are they?"

"Some of your ancestors," answered the Earl, "who lived a few hundred years ago."

"Perhaps," said Lord Fauntleroy, regarding them with respect, "perhaps I got my spelling from them." And then he proceeded to find his place in the church service. When the music began, he stood up and looked across at his mother, smiling. He was very fond of music, and his mother and he often sang together, so he joined in with the rest, his pure, sweet, high voice rising as clear as the song of a bird. He quite forgot himself in his pleasure in it. The Earl forgot himself a little too, as he sat in his curtain-shielded corner of the pew and watched the boy. His mother, as she looked at him across the church, felt a thrill pass through her heart, and a prayer rose in it too; a prayer that the pure, simple happiness of his childish soul might last, and that the strange, great fortune which had fallen to him might bring no wrong or evil with it. There were many soft anxious thoughts in her tender heart in those new days.

"Oh, Ceddie!" she had said to him the evening before, as she hung over him in saying good-night, before he went away; "Oh, Ceddie, dear, I wish for your sake I was very clever and could say a great many wise things! But only be good, dear, only be brave, only be kind and true always, and then you will never hurt any one so long as you live, and you may help many, and the big world may be better because my little child was born."

And on his return to the Castle, Fauntleroy had repeated her words to his grandfather.

"And I thought about you when she said that," he ended; "and I told her that was the way the world was because you had lived, and I was going to try if I could be like you."

"And what did she say to that?" asked his lordship, a trifle uneasily.

"She said that was right, and we must always look for good in people and try to be like it."

Perhaps it was this the old man remembered as he glanced through the divided folds of the red curtain of his pew to where his son's wife sat.

As they came out of the church, many of those who had attended the service stood waiting to see them pass. As they neared the gate, a man who stood with his hat in his hand made a step forward and then hesitated. He was a middle-aged farmer, with a careworn face.

"Well, Higgins," said the Earl.

Fauntleroy turned quickly to look at him.

"Oh!" he exclaimed; "is it Mr. Higgins?"

"Yes," answered the Earl dryly; "and I suppose he came to take a look at his new landlord."

"Yes, my lord," said the man, his sunburned face reddening. "Mr. Newick told me his young lordship was kind enough to speak for me, and I thought I'd like to say a word of thanks, if I might be allowed."

Perhaps he felt some wonder when he saw what a little fellow it was who had innocently done so much for him, and who stood there looking up just as one of his own less fortunate children might have done—apparently not realising his own importance in the least.

"I've a great deal to thank your lordship for," he said; "a great deal. I——"

"Oh," said Fauntleroy; "I only wrote the letter. It was my grandfather who did it. But you know how he is about always being good to everybody. Is Mrs. Higgins well now?"

Higgins looked a trifle taken aback. He also was somewhat startled at hearing his noble landlord presented in the character of a benevolent being, full of engaging qualities.

"I—well, yes, your lordship," he stammered.

"I'm glad of that," said Fauntleroy. "My grandfather was very sorry about your children having the scarlet fever, and so was I."

"You see, Higgins," broke in the Earl with a fine grim smile; "you people have been mistaken in me. Lord Fauntleroy understands me. Get into the carriage, Fauntleroy."

And Fauntleroy jumped in, and the carriage rolled away down the green lane, and even when it turned the corner into the high road, the Earl was still grimly smiling.

CHAPTER VIII.

LEARNING TO RIDE.

Lord Dorincourt had occasion to wear his grim smile many a time as the days passed by. Indeed, as his acquaintance with his grandson progressed, he wore the smile so often that there were moments when it almost lost its grimness. There is no denying that before Lord Fauntleroy had appeared on the scene, the old man had been growing very tired of his loneliness and his gout and his seventy years, but when he saw the lad, fortunately for the little fellow, the secret pride of the grandfather was gratified at the outset. And then when he heard the lad talk, and saw what a well-bred little fellow he was, notwithstanding his boyish ignorance of all that his new position meant, the old Earl liked his grandson more, and actually began to find himself rather entertained. It had amused him to give into those childish hands the power to bestow a benefit on poor Higgins. Then it had gratified him to drive to church with Cedric and to see the excitement and interest caused by the arrival. My lord of Dorincourt was an arrogant old man, proud of his name, proud of his rank, and therefore proud to show the world that at last the House of Dorincourt had an heir who was worthy of the position he was to fill.

The morning the new pony had been tried the Earl had been so pleased that he had almost forgotten his gout. When the groom had brought out the pretty creature, which arched its brown glossy neck and tossed its fine head in the sun, the Earl had sat at the open window of the library and had looked on while Fauntleroy took his first riding lesson. He wondered if the boy would show signs of timidity.

Fauntleroy mounted in great delight. He had never been on a pony before, and he was in the highest spirits. Wilkins, the groom, led the animal by the bridle up and down before the library window.

After a few minutes Fauntleroy spoke to his grandfather—watching him from the window.

"Can't I go myself?" he asked; "and can't I go faster?"

His lordship made a sign to Wilkins, who at the signal brought up his own horse and mounted it and took Fauntleroy's pony by the leading-rein.

"Now," said the Earl, "let him trot."

The next few minutes were rather exciting to the small equestrian. He found that trotting was not so easy as walking, and the faster the pony trotted, the less easy it was.

"It j-jolts a g-goo-good deal—do-doesn't it?" he said to Wilkins. "D-does it j-jolt y-you?"

"No, my lord," answered Wilkins. "You'll get used to it in time. Rise in your stirrups."

"I'm ri-rising all the t-time," said Fauntleroy.

He was both rising and falling rather uncomfortably and with many shakes and bounces. He was out of breath, but he held on with all his might, and sat as straight as he could. The Earl could see that from his window. When the riders came back within speaking distance, after they had been hidden by the trees a few minutes, Fauntleroy's hat was off, his cheeks were like poppies, and his lips were set, but he was still trotting manfully.

"Stop a minute!" said his grandfather. "Where's your hat?"

Wilkins touched his. "It fell off, your lordship," he said, with evident enjoyment. "Wouldn't let me stop to pick it up, my lord."

"Tired?" said the Earl to Fauntleroy. "Want to get off?"

"It jolts you more than you think it will," admitted his young lordship frankly. "And it tires you a little too; but I don't want to get off. I want to learn how. As soon as I've got my breath I want to go back for the hat."

The cleverest person in the world, if he had undertaken to teach Fauntleroy how to please the old man who watched him, could not have taught him anything which would have succeeded better. As the pony trotted off again toward the avenue, a faint colour crept up in the fierce old face, and the eyes, under the shaggy brows, gleamed with a pleasure such as his lordship had scarcely expected to know again. And he sat and watched quite eagerly until the sound of the horses' hoofs returned. When they did come, which was after some time, they came at a faster pace. Fauntleroy's hat was still off, Wilkins was carrying it for him; his cheeks were redder than before, and his hair was flying about his ears, but he came at quite a brisk canter.

"There!" he panted, as they drew up, "I c-cantered."

He and Wilkins and the pony were close friends after that. Scarcely a day passed on which the country people did not see them out together, cantering gaily on the highroad or through the green lanes. The children in the cottages would run to the door to look at the proud little brown pony with the gallant little figure sitting so straight in the saddle, and the young lord would snatch off his cap and swing it at them, and shout, "Hallo! Good morning!" in a very unlordly manner, though with great heartiness. Sometimes he would stop and talk with the children, and once Wilkins came back to the Castle with a story of how Fauntleroy had insisted on dismounting near the village school, so that a boy who was lame and tired might ride home on his pony.

"An' I'm blessed," said Wilkins, in telling the story at the stables,—"I'm blessed if he'd hear of anything else! He wouldn't let me get down, because he said the boy mightn't feel comfortable on a big horse. An' ses he, 'Wilkins,' ses he, 'that boy's lame and I'm not, and I want to talk to him too.' And up the lad has to get, and my lord trudges alongside of him with his hands in his pockets. And when we come to the cottage, an' the boy's mother comes out to see what's up, he whips off his cap an' ses he, 'I've brought your son home, ma'am,' ses he, 'because his leg hurt him, and I don't think that stick is enough for him to lean on; and I'm going to ask my grandfather to have a pair of crutches made for him.'"

When the Earl heard the story, he was not angry, as Wilkins had been half afraid that he would be; on the contrary, he laughed outright, and called Fauntleroy up to him, and made him tell all about the matter from beginning to end, and then he laughed again. And actually, a few days later, the Dorincourt carriage stopped in the green lane before the cottage where the lame boy lived, and Fauntleroy jumped out and walked up to the door, carrying a pair of strong, light, new crutches, and presented them to Mrs. Hartle (the lame boy's name was Hartle) with these words: "My grandfather's compliments, and if you please, these are for your boy, and we hope he will get better."

"I said your compliments," he explained to the Earl when he returned to the carriage. "You didn't tell me to, but I thought perhaps you forgot. That was right, wasn't it?"

And the Earl laughed again, and did not say it was not. In fact, the two were becoming more intimate every day, and every day Fauntleroy's faith in his lordship's benevolence and virtue increased. He had no doubt whatever that his grandfather was the most amiable and generous of elderly gentlemen. Certainly, he himself found his wishes gratified almost before they were uttered; and such gifts and pleasures were lavished upon him, that he was sometimes almost bewildered by his own possessions. Perhaps, notwithstanding his sweet nature, he might have been somewhat spoiled by it, if it had not been for the hours he spent with his mother at Court Lodge. That "best friend" of his watched over him very closely and tenderly. The two had many long talks together, and he never went back to the Castle with her kisses on his cheeks without carrying in his heart some simple, pure words worth remembering.

There was one thing, it is true, which puzzled the little fellow very much. He thought over the mystery of it much oftener than any one supposed; even his mother did not know how often he pondered on it; the Earl for a long time never suspected that he did so at all. But being quick to observe, the little boy could not help wondering why it was that his mother and grandfather never seemed to meet. He had noticed that they never did meet. And yet, every day, fruit and flowers were sent to Court Lodge from the hot-houses at the Castle. But the one virtuous action of the Earl's which had set him upon the pinnacle of perfection in Cedric's eyes, was what he had done soon after that first Sunday when Mrs. Errol had walked home from church unattended. About a week later, when Cedric was going one day to visit his mother, he found at the door, instead of the large carriage and prancing pair, a pretty little brougham and a handsome bay horse.

"That is a present from you to your mother," the Earl said abruptly. "She cannot go walking about the country. She needs a carriage. The man who drives will take charge of it. It is a present from you."

Fauntleroy's delight could but feebly express itself. He could scarcely contain himself until he reached the lodge. His mother was gathering roses in the garden. He flung himself out of the little brougham and flew to her.

"Dearest!" he cried, "could you believe it? This is yours! He says it is a present from me. It is your own carriage to drive everywhere in!"

He was so happy that she did not know what to say. She could not have borne to spoil his pleasure by refusing to accept the gift, even though it came from the man who chose to consider himself her enemy. She was obliged to step into the carriage, roses and all, and let herself be taken for a drive, while Fauntleroy told her stories of his grandfather's goodness and amiability. They were such innocent stories that sometimes she could not help laughing a little, and then she would draw her little boy closer to her side and kiss him, feeling glad that he could see only good in the old man who had so few friends.

The very next day after that, Fauntleroy wrote to Mr. Hobbs. He wrote quite a long letter, and after the first copy was written, he brought it to his grandfather to be inspected.

"Because," he said, "it's so uncertain about the spelling."

These were the last lines:

"I should like to see you and I wish dearest could live at the castle but I am very happy when I dont miss her too much and I love my granfarther every one does plees write soon

"your afechshnet old friend

"Cedric Errol.

"Do you miss your mother very much?" asked the Earl when he had finished reading this.

"Yes," said Fauntleroy, "I miss her all the time. And when I miss her very much, I go and look out of my window to where I see her light shine for me every night through an open place in the trees. It is a long way off, but she puts it in her window as soon as it is dark and I can see it twinkle far away, and I know what it says."

"What does it say?" asked my lord.

"It says, 'Good-night, God keep you all the night!'—just what she used to say when we were together. Every night she used to say that to me, and every morning she said, 'God bless you all the day!' So you see I am quite safe all the time——"

"Quite, I have no doubt," said his lordship dryly. And he drew down his beetling eyebrows and looked at the little boy so fixedly and so long that Fauntleroy wondered what he could be thinking of.

CHAPTER IX.

THE POOR COTTAGES.

The fact was, his lordship the Earl of Dorincourt thought in those days of many things of which he had never thought before, and all his thoughts were in one way or another connected with his grandson. His pride was the strongest part of his nature, and the boy gratified it at every point. Through this pride he began to find a new interest in life. He began to take pleasure in showing his heir to the world. The world had known of his disappointment in his sons; so there was an agreeable touch of triumph in exhibiting this new Lord Fauntleroy, who could disappoint no one. He made plans for his future. Sometimes in this new interest he forgot his gout, and after a while his doctor was surprised to find this noble patient's health growing better than he had expected it ever would be again. Perhaps the Earl grew better because the time did not pass so slowly for him, and he had something to think of besides his pains and infirmities.

One fine morning, people were amazed to see little Lord Fauntleroy riding his pony with another companion than Wilkins. This new companion rode a tall, powerful gray horse, and was no other than the Earl himself.

And in their rides together through the green lanes and pretty country roads, the two riders became more intimate than ever. And gradually the old man heard a great deal about "Dearest" and her life. As Fauntleroy trotted by the big horse he chatted gaily. There could not well have been a brighter little comrade, his nature was so happy. The Earl often was silent, listening and watching the joyous, glowing face. Sometimes he would tell his young companion to set the pony off at a gallop, and when the little fellow dashed off, sitting so straight and fearless, he would watch the boy with a gleam of pride and pleasure in his eyes; and Fauntleroy, when, after such a dash, he came back waving his cap with a laughing shout, always felt that he and his grandfather were very good friends indeed.

One thing that the Earl discovered was that his son's wife did not lead an idle life. It was not long before he learned that the poor people knew her very well indeed. When there was sickness or sorrow or poverty in any house, the little brougham often stood before the door.

It had not displeased the Earl to find that the mother of his heir had a beautiful young face and looked as much like a lady as if she had been a duchess, and in one way it did not displease him to know that she was popular and beloved by the poor. And yet he was often conscious of a hard, jealous pang when he saw how she filled her child's heart and how the boy clung to her as his best beloved. The old man would have desired to stand first himself and have no rival.

He felt it to be almost incredible that he, who had never really loved any one in his life, should find himself growing so fond of this little fellow,—as without doubt he was. At first he had only been pleased and proud of Cedric's beauty and bravery, but there was something more than pride in his feeling now. He laughed a grim, dry laugh all to himself sometimes, when he thought how he liked to have the boy near him, how he liked to hear his voice, and how in secret he really wished to be liked and thought well of by his small grandson.

It was only about a week after that ride when, after a visit to his mother, Fauntleroy came into the library with a troubled, thoughtful face. He sat down in that high-backed chair in which he had sat on the evening of his arrival, and for a while he looked at the embers on the hearth. The Earl watched him in silence, wondering what was coming. It was evident that Cedric had something on his mind. At last he looked up "Does Newick know all about the people?" he asked.

"It is his business to know about them," said his lordship. "Been neglecting it—has he?"

Contradictory as it may seem, there was nothing which entertained and edified him more than the little fellow's interest in his tenantry.

"There is a place," said Fauntleroy, looking up at him with wide-open, horror-stricken eyes—"Dearest has seen it; it is at the other end of the village. The houses are close together, and almost falling down; you can scarcely breathe: and the people are so poor, and everything is dreadful! The rain comes in at the roof! Dearest went to see a poor woman who lived there. The tears ran down her cheeks when she told me about it!"

The tears had come into his own eyes, but he smiled through them.

"I told her you didn't know, and I would tell you," he said. He jumped down and came and leaned against the Earl's chair. "You can make it all right," he said, "just as you made it all right for Higgins. You always make it all right for everybody. I told her you would, and that Newick must have forgotten to tell you."

The Earl looked down at the hand on his knee. Newick had not forgotten to tell him; in fact, Newick had spoken to him more than once of the desperate condition of the end of the village known as Earl's Court. Mr. Mordaunt had painted it all to him in the strongest words he could use, and his lordship had used violent language in response; and, when his gout had been at the worst, he had said that the sooner the people of Earl's Court died and were buried by the parish the better it would be—and there was an end of the matter. And yet, as he looked at the small hand on his knee, and from the small hand to the honest, earnest, frank-eyed face, he was actually ashamed both of Earl's Court and of himself.

"What!" he said; "you want to make a builder of model cottages of me, do you?" And he positively put his own hand upon the childish one and stroked it.

"Those must be pulled down," said Fauntleroy, with great eagerness. "Dearest says so. Let us—let us go and have them pulled down to-morrow. The people will be so glad when they see you! They'll know you have come to help them!" And his eyes shone like stars in his glowing face.

The Earl rose from his chair and put his hand on the child's shoulder. "Let us go out and take our walk on the terrace," he said, with a short laugh; "and we can talk it over."

And though he laughed two or three times again, as they walked to and fro on the broad stone terrace, where they walked together almost every fine evening, he seemed to be thinking of something which did not displease him, and still he kept his hand on his small companion's shoulder.

CHAPTER X.

THE EARL ALARMED.

The truth was that Mrs. Errol had found a great many sad things in the course of her work among the poor of the little village that appeared so picturesque when it was seen from the moor-sides. Everything was not as picturesque when seen near by, as it looked from a distance. She had found idleness and poverty and ignorance where there should have been comfort and industry. And she had discovered, after a while, that Erlesboro was considered to be the worst village in that part of the country.

As to Earl's Court, it was a disgrace, with its dilapidated houses and miserable, careless, sickly people. When first Mrs. Errol went to the place, it made her shudder. And a bold thought came into her wise little mother-heart. Gradually she had begun to see, as had others, that it had been her boy's good fortune to please the Earl very much, and that he would scarcely be likely to be denied anything for which he expressed a desire.

"The Earl would give him anything," she said to Mr. Mordaunt. "He would indulge his every whim. Why should not that indulgence be used for the good of others? It is for me to see that this shall come to pass."

She knew she could trust the kind, childish heart; so she told the little fellow the story of Earl's Court, feeling sure that he would speak of it to his grandfather, and hoping that some good results would follow.

And strange as it appeared to every one, good results did follow. The fact was that the strongest power to influence the Earl was his grandson's perfect confidence in him—the fact that Cedric always believed that his grandfather was going to do what was right and generous. He could not quite make up his mind to let him discover that he had no inclination to be generous at all, and so after some reflection, he sent for Newick, and had quite a long interview with him on the subject of the Court, and it was decided that the wretched hovels should be pulled down and new houses should be built.

"It is Lord Fauntleroy who insists on it," he said dryly; "he thinks it will improve the property. You can tell the tenants that it's his idea."

Of course, both the country people and the town people heard of the proposed improvement. At first, many of them would not believe it; but when a small army of workmen arrived and commenced pulling down the crazy, squalid cottages, people began to understand that little Lord Fauntleroy had done them a good turn again, and that through his innocent interference the scandal of Earl's Court had at last been removed.

When the cottages were being built, the lad and his grandfather used to ride over to Earl's Court together to look at them, and Fauntleroy was full of interest. He would dismount from his pony and go and make acquaintance with the workmen, asking them questions about building and bricklaying and telling them things about America.

When he left them, the workmen used to talk him over among themselves, and laugh at his odd, innocent speeches; but they liked him, and liked to see him stand among them, talking away, with his hands in his pockets, his hat pushed back on his curls, and his small face full of eagerness. And they would go home and tell their wives about him, and the women would tell each other, and so it came about that almost every one talked of, or knew some story of, little Lord Fauntleroy; and gradually almost every one knew that the "wicked Earl" had found something he cared for at last—something which had touched and even warmed his hard, bitter old heart.

But no one knew quite how much it had been warmed, and how day by day the old man found himself caring more and more for the child, who was the only creature that had ever trusted him.

He never spoke to any one else of his feeling for Cedric; when he spoke of him to others it was always with the same grim smile. But Fauntleroy soon knew that his grandfather loved him and always liked him to be near—near to his chair if they were in the library, opposite to him at table, or by his side when he rode or drove or took his evening walk on the broad terrace.

"Do you remember," Cedric said once looking up from his book as he lay on the rug, "do you remember what I said to you that first night about our being good companions? I don't think any people could be better friends than we are, do you?"

"We are pretty good companions, I should say," replied his lordship. "Come here."

Fauntleroy scrambled up and went to him.

"Is there anything you want," the Earl asked; "anything you have not?"

The little fellow's brown eyes fixed themselves on his grandfather with a rather wistful look.

"Only one thing," he answered.

"What is that?" inquired the Earl.

Fauntleroy was silent a second. He had not thought matters over to himself so long for nothing.

"What is it?" my lord repeated.

Fauntleroy answered.

"It is Dearest," he said.

The old Earl winced a little.

"But you see her almost every day," he said. "Is not that enough?"

"I used to see her all the time," said Fauntleroy. "She used to kiss me when I went to sleep at night, and in the morning she was always there, and we could tell each other things without waiting."

The old eyes and the young ones looked into each other through a moment of silence. Then the Earl knitted his brows.

"Do you never forget about your mother?" he said.

"No," answered Fauntleroy, "never; and she never forgets about me. I shouldn't forget about you, you know, if I didn't live with you. I should think about you all the more."

"Upon my word," said the Earl, after looking at him a moment longer, "I believe you would!"

The jealous pang that came when the boy spoke so of his mother seemed even stronger than it had been before—it was stronger because of this old man's increasing affection for the boy.

But it was not long before he had other pangs, so much harder to face that he almost forgot, for the time, he had ever hated his son's wife at all. And in a strange and startling way it happened. One evening, just before the Earl's Court cottages were completed, there was a grand dinner party at Dorincourt. There had not been such a party at the Castle for a long time. A few days before it took place, Sir Harry Lorridaile and Lady Lorridaile, who was the Earl's only sister, actually came for a visit—a thing which caused the greatest excitement in the village and set Mrs. Dibble's shop-bell tinkling madly again, because it was well known that Lady Lorridaile had only been to Dorincourt once since her marriage, thirty-five years before. She was a handsome old lady with white curls and dimpled, peachy cheeks, and she was as good as gold, but she had never approved of her brother any more than did the rest of the world, and having a strong will of her own and not being at all afraid to speak her mind frankly, she had, after several lively quarrels with his lordship, seen very little of him since her young days.

Not only the poor people and farmers heard about little Lord Fauntleroy; others knew of him. He was talked about so much and there were so many stories of him—of his beauty, his sweet temper, his popularity, and his growing influence over the Earl his grandfather—that rumours of him reached the gentry at their country places and he was heard of in more than one county of England.

And so by degrees Lady Lorridaile, too, heard of the child; she heard about Higgins, and the lame boy, and the cottages at Earl's Court, and a score of other things,—and she began to wish to see the little fellow. And just as she was wondering how it might be brought about, to her utter astonishment, she received a letter from her brother inviting her to come with her husband to Dorincourt.

"It seems incredible!" she exclaimed. "I have heard it said that the child has worked miracles, and I begin to believe it. They say my brother adores the boy and can scarcely endure to have him out of sight. And he is so proud of him! Actually, I believe he wants to show him to us." And she accepted the invitation at once.

When she reached Dorincourt Castle with Sir Harry, it was late in the afternoon, and she went to her room at once before seeing her brother. Having dressed for dinner she entered the drawing-room. The Earl was there standing near the fire and looking very tall and imposing; and at his side stood a little boy in black velvet, and a large Vandyke collar of rich lace—a little fellow whose round bright face was so handsome, and who turned upon her such beautiful, candid brown eyes, that she almost uttered an exclamation of pleasure and surprise at the sight.

As she shook hands with the Earl, she called him by the name she had not used since her girl-hood.

"What, Molyneux," she said, "is this the child?"

"Yes, Constantia," answered the Earl, "this is the boy. Fauntleroy, this is your grand-aunt, Lady Lorridaile."

"How do you do, grand-aunt?" said Fauntleroy.

Lady Lorridaile put her hand on his shoulder, and after looking down into his upraised face a few seconds, kissed him warmly.

"I am your Aunt Constantia," she said, "and I loved your poor papa, and you are very like him."

"It makes me glad when I am told I am like him," answered Fauntleroy, "because it seems as if every one liked him,—just like Dearest, eszackly,—Aunt Constantia," (adding the two words after a second's pause).

Lady Lorridaile was delighted. She bent and kissed him again, and from that moment they were warm friends.

"Well, Molyneux," she said aside to the Earl afterwards, "it could not possibly be better than this!"

"I think not," answered his lordship dryly. "He is a fine little fellow. We are great friends. He believes me to be the most charming and sweet-tempered of philanthropists. I will confess to you, Constantia,—as you would find it out if I did not,—that I am in some slight danger of becoming rather an old fool about him."

"What does his mother think of you?" asked Lady Lorridaile, with her usual straightforwardness.

"I have not asked her," answered the Earl, slightly scowling.

"Well," said Lady Lorridaile, "I will be frank with you at the outset, Molyneux, and tell you I don't approve of your course, and that it is my intention to call on Mrs. Errol as soon as possible; so if you wish to quarrel with me, you had better mention it at once. What I hear of the young creature makes me quite sure that her child owes her everything. We were told even at Lorridaile Park that your poorer tenants adore her already."

"They adore him," said the Earl, nodding towards Fauntleroy. "As to Mrs. Errol, you'll find her a pretty little woman. I'm rather in debt to her for giving some of her beauty to the boy, and you can go to see her if you like. All I ask is that she will remain at Court Lodge and that you will not ask me to go and see her," and he scowled a little again.

"But he doesn't hate her as much as he used to, that is plain enough to me," her ladyship said to Sir Harry afterwards. "And he is a changed man in a measure, and, incredible as it may seem, Harry, it is my opinion that he is being made into a human being, through nothing more or less than his affection for that innocent, affectionate little fellow."

The very next day she went to call upon Mrs. Errol. When she returned, she said to her brother:

"Molyneux, she is the loveliest little woman I ever saw! She has a voice like a silver bell, and you may thank her for making the boy what he is. She has given him more than her beauty, and you make a great mistake in not persuading her to come and take charge of you. I shall invite her to Lorridaile."

"She'll not leave the boy," replied the Earl.

"I must have the boy too," said Lady Lorridaile, laughing.

But she knew Fauntleroy would not be given up to her, and each day she saw more clearly how closely those two had grown to each other, and how all the proud, grim old man's ambition and hope and love centred themselves in the child, and how the warm, innocent nature returned his affection with most perfect trust and good faith.

She knew, too, that the prime reason for the great dinner party was the Earl's secret desire to show the world his grandson and heir. Perhaps there was not one person who accepted the invitation without feeling some curiosity about little Lord Fauntleroy, and wondering if he would be on view.

And when the time came he was on view.

"The lad has good manners," said the Earl. "He will be in no one's way. He can actually answer when he's spoken to, and be silent when he is not."

But he was not allowed to be silent very long. Every one had something to say to him. The fact was they wished to make him talk. The ladies petted him and asked him questions, and the men asked him questions too, and joked with him, as the men on the steamer had done when he crossed the Atlantic.

But though he was talked to so much, as the Earl had said, he was in no one's way. He could be quiet and listen when others talked, and so no one found him tiresome.

Mr. Havisham had been expected to arrive in the afternoon, but, strange to say, he was late. Such a thing had really never been known to happen before during all the years in which he had been a visitor at Dorincourt Castle. He was so late that the guests were on the point of rising to go in to dinner when he arrived. When he approached his host, the Earl regarded him with amazement. He looked as if he had been hurried or agitated; his dry, keen old face was actually pale.

"I was detained," he said, in a low voice to the Earl, "by—an extraordinary event."

It was as unlike the methodic old lawyer to be agitated by anything as it was to be late, but it was evident that he had been disturbed. At dinner he ate scarcely anything, and two or three times, when he was spoken to, he started as if his thoughts were far away. At dessert, when Fauntleroy came in, he looked at him more than once, nervously and uneasily. Fauntleroy noted the look and wondered at it. He and Mr. Havisham were on friendly terms, and they usually exchanged smiles.

The lawyer seemed to have forgotten to smile that evening.

He did not exactly know how the long, superb dinner ended. He sat through it as if he were in a dream, and several times he saw the Earl glance at him in surprise.

But it was over at last, and the gentlemen joined the ladies in the drawing-room. They found Fauntleroy sitting on a sofa with Miss Vivian Herbert,—the great beauty of the last London season; they had been looking at some pictures, and he was thanking his companion, as the door opened.

"I'm ever so much obliged to you for being so kind to me!" he was saying; "I never was at a party before, and I've enjoyed myself so much!"

He had enjoyed himself so much that his eyelids began to droop. He was quite sure he was not going to sleep, but there was a large, yellow satin cushion behind him and his head sank against it, and after a while his eyelids drooped for the last time.

No sooner had the last guest left the room, than Mr. Havisham turned from his place by the fire, and stepped nearer the sofa, where he stood looking down at the sleeping occupant.

"Well, Havisham," said the Earl's harsh voice behind him. "What is it? It is evident something has happened. What was the extraordinary event, if I may ask?"

Mr. Havisham turned from the sofa, still rubbing his chin.

"It was bad news," he answered, "distressing news, my lord—the worst of news. I am sorry to be the bearer of it."

The Earl had been uneasy for some time during the evening, as he glanced at Mr. Havisham, and when he was uneasy he was always ill-tempered.

"Why do you look so at the boy!" he exclaimed irritably. "You have been looking at him all the evening as if—. What has your news to do with Lord Fauntleroy?"

"My lord," said Mr. Havisham, "I will waste no words. My news has everything to do with Lord Fauntleroy. And if we are to believe it—it is not Lord Fauntleroy who lies sleeping before us, but only the son of Captain Errol. And the present Lord Fauntleroy is the son of your son Bevis, and is at this moment in a lodging-house in London."

The Earl clutched the arms of his chair with both his hands until the veins stood out upon them; the veins stood out on his forehead too; his fierce old face was almost livid.

"What do you mean!" he cried out. "You are mad! Whose lie is this?"

"If it is a lie," answered Mr. Havisham, "it is painfully like the truth. A woman came to my chambers this morning. She said your son Bevis married her six years ago in London. She showed me her marriage certificate. They quarrelled a year after the marriage, and he paid her to keep away from him. She has a son five years old. She is an American of the lower classes,—an ignorant person,—and until lately she did not fully understand what her son could claim. She consulted a lawyer, and found out that the boy was really Lord

Fauntleroy and the heir to the earldom of Dorincourt; and she, of course, insists on his claims being acknowledged.”

The handsome, grim old face was ghastly. A bitter smile fixed itself upon it.

“I should refuse to believe a word of it,” he said, “if it were not such a low, scoundrelly piece of business that it becomes quite possible in connection with the name of my son Bevis. It is quite like Bevis. He was always a disgrace to us. The woman is an ignorant, vulgar person, you say?”

“I am obliged to admit that she can scarcely spell her own name,” answered the lawyer. “She cares for nothing but the money. She is very handsome in a coarse way, but——”

The fastidious old lawyer ceased speaking and gave a sort of shudder.

The veins on the old Earl’s forehead stood out like purple cords. Something else stood out upon it too—cold drops of moisture. He took out his handkerchief and swept them away. His smile grew even more bitter.

“And I,” he said, “I objected to—to the other woman, the mother of this child” (pointing to the sleeping form on the sofa); “I refused to recognize her. And yet she could spell her own name. I suppose this is retribution.”

Suddenly he sprang up from his chair and began to walk up and down the room. Fierce and terrible words poured forth from his lips. His rage and hatred and cruel disappointment shook him as a storm shakes a tree.

“I might have known it,” he said. “They were a disgrace to me from their first hour! I hated them both; and they hated me! Bevis was the worse of the two. I will not believe this yet though! I will contend against it to the last. But it is like Bevis—it is like him!”

And then he raged again and asked questions about the woman, about her proofs, and pacing the room, turned first white and then purple in his repressed fury.

When at last he had learned all that was to be told, and knew the worst, Mr. Havisham looked at him with a feeling of anxiety. He looked broken and haggard and changed. His rages had always been bad for him, but this one had been worse than the rest because there had been something more than rage in it.

He came slowly back to the sofa, at last, and stood near it.

"If any one had told me I could be fond of a child," he said, his harsh voice low and unsteady, "I should not have believed them. I always detested children—my own more than the rest. I am fond of this one; he is fond of me" (with a bitter smile). "I am not popular; I never was. But he is fond of me. He never was afraid of me—he always trusted me. He would have filled my place better than I have filled it. I know that. He would have been an honour to the name."

He bent down and stood a minute or so looking at the happy, sleeping face. He put up his hand, pushed the bright hair back from the forehead, and then turned away and rang the bell.

When the footman appeared, he pointed to the sofa.

"Take"—he said, and then his voice changed a little—"take Lord Fauntleroy to his room."

CHAPTER XI.

ANXIETY IN AMERICA.

When Mr. Hobbs's young friend left him to go to Dorincourt Castle and become Lord Fauntleroy, and the grocery-man had time to realise that the Atlantic Ocean lay between himself and the small companion who had spent so many agreeable hours in his society, he began to feel very lonely indeed. At first it seemed to Mr. Hobbs that Cedric was not really far away, and would come back again; that some day he would look up from his paper and see the lad standing in the doorway, in his white suit and red stockings, and with his straw hat on the back of his head, and would hear him say in his cheerful little voice: "Hello, Mr. Hobbs! This is a hot day—isn't it?" But as the days passed on and this did not happen, Mr. Hobbs felt very dull and uneasy. He did not even enjoy his newspaper as much as he used to. He would take out his gold watch and open it and stare at the inscription; "From his oldest friend, Lord Fauntleroy, to Mr. Hobbs. When this you see, remember me." At night, when the store was closed, he would light his pipe and walk slowly along until he reached the house where Cedric had lived, on which there was a sign that read, "This House to Let"; and he would stop near it and look up and shake his head, and puff at his pipe very hard, and after a while walk mournfully back again.

This went on for two or three weeks before a new idea came to him. He would go to see Dick. He smoked a great many pipes before he arrived at the conclusion, but finally he did arrive at it. He would go to see Dick. He knew all about Dick. Cedric had told him, and his idea was that perhaps Dick might be some comfort to him in the way of talking things over.

So one day when Dick was very hard at work blacking a customer's boots, a short, stout man with a heavy face and a bald head, stared for two or three minutes at the bootblack's sign, which read:

"Professor Dick Tipton

Can't be beat."

He stared at it so long that Dick began to take a lively interest in him, and when he had put the finishing touch to his customer's boots, he said:

"Want a shine, sir?"

The stout man came forward deliberately and put his foot on the rest.

"Yes," he said.

Then when Dick fell to work, the stout man looked from Dick to the sign and from the sign to Dick.

"Where did you get that?" he asked.

"From a friend o' mine," said Dick,—"a little feller. He was the best little feller ye ever saw. He's in England now. Gone to be one o' those lords."

"Lord—Lord—" asked Mr. Hobbs, with ponderous slowness, "Lord Fauntleroy—Goin' to be Earl of Dorincourt!"

Dick almost dropped his brush.

"Why, boss!" he exclaimed, "d'ye know him yerself?"

"I've known him," answered Mr. Hobbs, wiping his warm forehead, "ever since he was born. We were lifetime acquaintances—that's what we were."

It really made him feel quite agitated to speak of it. He pulled the splendid gold watch out of his pocket and opened it, and showed the inside of the case to Dick.

"'When this you see, remember me,'" he read. "That was his parting keepsake to me. I'd ha' remembered him," he went on, shaking his head, "if he hadn't given me a thing. He was a companion as any man would remember."

It proved that they had so much to say to each other that it was not possible to say it all at one time, and so it was agreed that the next night Dick should make a visit to the store and keep Mr. Hobbs company.

This was the beginning of quite a substantial friendship. When Dick went up to the store, Mr. Hobbs received him with great hospitality. He gave him a chair tilted against the door, near a barrel of apples, and after his young visitor was seated, he made a jerk at them with the hand in which he held his pipe, saying:

"Help yerself."

Then they read, and discussed the British aristocracy; and Mr. Hobbs smoked his pipe very hard and shook his head a great deal.

He seemed to derive a great deal of comfort from Dick's visit. Before Dick went home, they had a supper in the small back room; they had biscuits and cheese and sardines, and other things out of the store, and Mr. Hobbs solemnly opened two bottles of ginger ale, and pouring out two glasses, proposed a toast.

"Here's to him!" he said, lifting his glass, "an' may he teach 'em a lesson—earls an' markises an' dooks an' all!"

After that night, the two saw each other often, and Mr. Hobbs was much more comfortable and less desolate. They read the Penny Story Gazette, and many other interesting things, and gained a knowledge of the habits of the nobility and gentry which would have surprised those despised classes if they had realised it. One day Mr. Hobbs made a pilgrimage to a book-store down town, for the express purpose of adding to their library. He went to a clerk and leaned over the counter to speak to him.

"I want," he said, "a book about earls."

"What!" exclaimed the clerk.

"A book," repeated the grocery-man, "about earls."

"I'm afraid," said the clerk, looking rather queer, "that we haven't what you want."

"Haven't?" said Mr. Hobbs, anxiously. "Well, say markises then—or dooks."

"I know of no such book," answered the clerk.

Mr. Hobbs was much disturbed. He looked down on the floor,—then he looked up.

"None about female earls?" he inquired.

"I'm afraid not," said the clerk, with a smile.

"Well," exclaimed Mr. Hobbs, "I'll be jiggered!"

He was just going out of the store, when the clerk called him back and asked him if a story in which the nobility were chief characters would do. Mr. Hobbs said it would—if he could not get an entire volume devoted to earls. So the clerk sold him a book called The Tower of London, written by Mr. Harrison Ainsworth, and he carried it home.

When Dick came they began to read it. It was a very wonderful and exciting book, and the scene was laid in the reign of the famous English queen who is called by some people Bloody Mary. And as Mr. Hobbs heard of Queen Mary's deeds and the habit she had of chopping people's heads off, putting them to the torture, and burning them alive, he became very much excited. He took his pipe out of his mouth and stared at Dick.

"Why, he ain't safe!" he said. "He ain't safe! If the women folks can sit up on their thrones an' give the word for things like that to be done, who's to know what's happening to him this very minute?"

"Well," said Dick, though he looked rather anxious himself; "ye see this 'ere un isn't the one that's bossin' things now. I know her name's Victory, an' this un here in the book,— her name's Mary."

"So it is," said Mr. Hobbs, still mopping his forehead; "so it is,—but still it doesn't seem as if 'twas safe for him over there with those queer folks. Why, they tell me they don't keep the Fourth o' July!"

He was privately uneasy for several days; and it was not until he received Fauntleroy's letter and had read it several times, both to himself and to Dick, and had also read the letter Dick got about the same time, that he became composed again.

But they both found great pleasure in their letters. They read and re-read them, and talked them over and enjoyed every word of them. And they spent days over the answers they sent, and read them over almost as often as the letters they had received.

One day they were sitting in the store doorway together, and Mr. Hobbs was filling his pipe, whilst Dick told him all about his life and his elder brother, who had been very good to him after their parents had died. The brother's name was Ben, and he had managed to get quite a decent place in a store. "And then," said Dick, "blest if he didn't go an' marry a gal, a regular tiger-cat. She'd tear things to pieces, when she got mad. Had a baby just like her; 'n' at last Ben went out West with a man to set up a cattle ranch."

"He oughtn't to 've married," Mr. Hobbs said solemnly, as he rose to get a match.

As he took the match from its box, he stopped and looked down on the counter.

"Why!" he said, "if here isn't a letter! I didn't see it afore. The postman must have laid it down when I wasn't noticin', or the newspaper slipped over it."

He picked it up and looked at it carefully.

"It's from him!" he exclaimed. "That's the very one it's from!"

He forgot his pipe altogether. He went back to his chair quite excited, and took his pocket-knife and opened the envelope.

"I wonder what news there is this time," he said.

And then he unfolded the letter and read as follows:

"Dorincourt Castle.

"My dear Mr. Hobbs.

"I write this in a great hury becaus i have something curous to tell you i know you will be very mutch suprised my dear frend when i tel you. It is all a mistake and i am not a lord and i shall not have to be an earl there is a lady whitch was marid to my uncle bevis who is dead and she has a little boy and he is lord fauntleroy becaus that is the way it is in England and my name is Cedric Errol like it was when I was in New York and all the things will belong to the other boy i thought at first i should have to give him my pony and cart but my grandfarther says i need not my grandfarther is very sorry i am not rich now becaus when your papa is only the youngest son he is not very rich i am going to learn to work so that I can take care of dearest i have been asking Wilkins about grooming horses preaps i might be a groom or a coachman. I thort i would tell you and Dick right away becaus you would be intrusted so no more at present with love from

"your old frend

"Cedric Errol (Not lord Fauntleroy)."

Mr. Hobbs fell back in his chair, the letter dropped on his knee, his penknife slipped to the floor, and so did the envelope.

"Well!" he ejaculated, "I am jiggered!"

He was so dumfounded that he actually changed his exclamation. It had always been his habit to say, "I will be jiggered," but this time he said, "I am jiggered." Perhaps he really was jiggered. There is no knowing.

"Well," said Mr. Hobbs. "It's my opinion it's all a put-up job o' the British 'ristycrats to rob him of his rights because he's an American. They're trying to rob him! that's what they're doing, and folks that have money ought to look after him."

And he kept Dick with him until quite a late hour to talk it over, and when that young man left he went with him to the corner of the street; and on his way back he stopped opposite the empty house for some time, staring at the "To Let," and smoking his pipe in much disturbance of mind.

CHAPTER XII.

THE RIVAL CLAIMANTS.

A very few days after the dinner-party at the Castle, almost everybody in England who read the newspaper at all knew the romantic story of what had happened at Dorincourt. It made a very interesting story when it was told with all the details. There was the little American boy who had been brought to England to be Lord Fauntleroy, and who was said to be so fine and handsome a little fellow, and to have already made people fond of him; there was the old Earl, his grandfather, who was so proud of his heir; there was the pretty young mother who had never been forgiven for marrying Captain Errol; and there was the strange marriage of Bevis the dead Lord Fauntleroy, and the strange wife, of whom no one knew anything, suddenly appearing with her son, and saying that he was the real Lord Fauntleroy and must have his rights. All these things were talked about and written about, and caused a tremendous sensation. And then there came the rumour that the Earl of Dorincourt was not satisfied with the turn affairs had taken, and would perhaps contest the claim by law, and the matter might end with a wonderful trial.

There never had been such excitement before in the county in which Erlesboro was situated. On market-days, people stood in groups and talked and wondered what would be done; the farmers' wives invited one another to tea that they might tell one another all they had heard and all they thought and all they thought other people thought.

In fact there was excitement everywhere; at the Castle, in the library, where the Earl and Mr. Havisham sat and talked; in the servants' hall, where Mr. Thomas and the butler and the other men and women servants gossiped and exclaimed at all times of the day; and in the stables, where Wilkins went about his work in a quite depressed state of mind.

But in the midst of all the disturbance there was one person who was quite calm and untroubled. That person was the little Lord Fauntleroy who was said not to be Lord Fauntleroy at all. When first the Earl told him what had happened, he had sat on a stool holding on to his knee, as he so often did when he was listening to anything interesting; and by the time the story was finished, he looked quite sober.

"It makes me feel very queer," he said; "it makes me—queer!"

The Earl looked at the boy in silence. It made him feel queer too—queerer than he had ever felt in his whole life. And he felt more queer still when he saw that there was a troubled expression on the small face which was usually so happy.

"Will they take Dearest's house away from her—and her carriage?" Cedric asked in a rather unsteady, anxious little voice.

"No!" said the Earl decidedly—in quite a loud voice in fact. "They can take nothing from her."

"Ah!" said Cedric with evident relief. "Can't they?"

Then he looked up at his grandfather, and there was a wistful shade in his eyes, and they looked very big and soft.

"That other boy," he said rather tremulously—"he will have to—to be your boy now—as I was—won't he?"

"No!" answered the Earl—and he said it so fiercely and loudly that Cedric quite jumped.

"No?" he exclaimed, in wonderment. "Won't he? I thought——"

He stood up from his stool quite suddenly.

"Shall I be your boy, even if I'm not going to be an earl?" he said. "Shall I be your boy, just as I was before?" And his flushed little face was all alight with eagerness.

How the old Earl did look at him from head to foot, to be sure! How his great shaggy brows did draw themselves together, and how queerly his deep eyes shone under them— how very queerly!

"My boy!" he said "yes, you'll be my boy as long as I live; and, by George, sometimes I feel as if you were the only boy I had ever had."

Cedric's face turned red to the roots of his hair; it turned red with relief and pleasure. He put both his hands deep into his pockets and looked squarely into his noble relative's eyes.

"Do you?" he said. "Well, then, I don't care about the earl part at all. I don't care whether

I'm an earl or not. I thought—you see, I thought the one that was going to be the Earl would have to be your boy too, and—and I couldn't be. That was what made me feel so queer."

The Earl put his hand on his shoulder and drew him nearer.

"They shall take nothing from you that I can hold for you," he said, drawing his breath hard. "I won't believe yet that they can take anything from you. You were made for the place, and—well, you may fill it still. But whatever comes, you shall have all that I can give you—all!"

It scarcely seemed as if he were speaking to a child, there was such determination in his face and voice; it was more as if he were making a promise to himself—and perhaps he was.

He had never before known how deep a hold upon him his fondness for the boy and his pride in him had taken. He had never seen his strength and good qualities and beauty as he seemed to see them now. To his obstinate nature it seemed impossible—to give up what he had so set his heart upon. And he had determined that he would not give it up without a fierce struggle.

Within a few days after she had seen Mr. Havisham, the woman who claimed to be Lady Fauntleroy presented herself at the Castle, and brought her child with her. She was sent away. The Earl would not see her, she was told by the footman at the door; his lawyer would attend to her cause.

Mr. Havisham had noticed, during his interviews with her, that she was neither so clever nor so bold as she meant to be. It was as if she had not expected to meet with such opposition.

"She is evidently," the lawyer said to Mrs. Errol, "a person from the lower walks of life. She is uneducated and quite unused to meeting people like ourselves on any terms of equality. She does not know what to do. Her visit to the Castle quite cowed her. She was infuriated, but she was cowed. The Earl would not receive her, but I advised him to go with me to the Dorincourt Arms, where she is staying. When she saw him enter the room, she turned white, though she flew into a rage at once, and threatened and demanded in one breath."

The fact was that the Earl had stalked into the room and stood, looking like a venerable aristocratic giant, staring at the woman and not condescending a word. He let her talk and demand until she was tired, without himself uttering a word, and then he said:

"You say you are my eldest son's wife. If that is true, and if the proof you offer is too much for us, the law is on your side. In that case, your boy is Lord Fauntleroy. If your claims are proved, you will be provided for. I want to see nothing either of you or the child so long as I live."

And then he turned his back upon her and stalked out of the room as he had stalked into it.

Not many days after that, a visitor was announced to Mrs. Errol, who was writing in her little morning room. The maid who brought the message looked rather excited.

"It's the Earl hisself, ma'am!" she said in tremulous awe.

When Mrs. Errol entered the drawing-room, a very tall, majestic-looking old man was standing on the tiger-skin rug. He had a handsome, grim old face, with an aquiline profile, a long white moustache, and an obstinate look.

"Mrs. Errol, I believe?" he said.

"Mrs. Errol," she answered.

"I am the Earl of Dorincourt," he said.

He paused a moment, almost unconsciously, to look into her uplifted eyes. They were so like the big, affectionate, childish eyes he had seen uplifted to his own so often every day during the last few months, that they gave him a quite curious sensation.

"The boy is very like you," he said abruptly.

"It has been often said so, my lord," she replied, "but I have been glad to think him like his father also."

As Lady Lorridaile had told him, her voice was very sweet, and her manner was very simple and dignified. She did not seem in the least troubled by his sudden coming.

"Yes," said the Earl, "he is like—my son—too." He put his hand up to his big white moustache and pulled it fiercely. "Do you know," he said, "why I have come here?"

"I have seen Mr. Havisham," Mrs. Errol began, "and he has told me of the claims which have been made——"

"I have come to tell you," said the Earl, "that they will be investigated and contested, if a contest can be made. I have come to tell you that the boy shall be defended with all the power of the law. His rights——"

The soft voice interrupted him.

"He must have nothing that is not his by right, even if the law can give it to him," she said.

"Unfortunately the law cannot," said the Earl. "If it could, it should. This outrageous woman and her child——"

"Perhaps she cares for him as much as I care for Cedric, my lord," said little Mrs. Errol. "And if she was your eldest son's wife, her son is Lord Fauntleroy, and mine is not."

"I suppose," said the Earl, "that you would much prefer that he should not be the Earl of Dorincourt?"

Her fair young face flushed.

"It is a very magnificent thing to be the Earl of Dorincourt, my lord," she said. "I know that, but I care most that he should be what his father was—brave and just and true always."

"In striking contrast to what his grandfather was, eh?" said his lordship sardonically.

"I have not had the pleasure of knowing his grandfather," replied Mrs. Errol, "but I know my little boy believes——" She stopped short a moment, looking quietly into his face, and then she added, "I know that Cedric loves you."

"Would he have loved me," said the Earl dryly, "if you had told him why I did not receive you at the Castle?"

"No," answered Mrs. Errol; "I think not. That was why I did not wish him to know."

"Well," said my lord, brusquely, "there are few women who would not have told him."

He suddenly began to walk up and down the room, pulling his great moustache more violently than ever.

"Yes, he is fond of me," he said, "and I am fond of him. I can't say I ever was fond of anything before. I am fond of him. He pleased me from the first. I am an old man, and was tired of my life. He has given me something to live for. I am proud of him. I was satisfied to think of his taking his place some day as the head of the family."

He came back and stood before Mrs. Errol.

"I am miserable," he said. "Miserable!"

He looked as if he was. Even his pride could not keep his voice steady or his hands from shaking. For a moment it almost seemed as if his deep, fierce eyes had tears in them. "Perhaps it is because I am miserable that I have come to you," he said, quite glaring down at her. "I used to hate you; I have been jealous of you. This wretched, disgraceful business has changed that. I have been an obstinate old fool, and I suppose I have treated you badly. You are like the boy and the boy is the first object in my life. I am miserable, and I came to you merely because you are like the boy, and he cares for you, and I care for him. Treat me as well as you can, for the boy's sake."

He said it all in his harsh voice, and almost roughly, but somehow he seemed so broken down for the time that Mrs. Errol was touched to the heart. She got up and moved an arm-chair a little forward.

"I wish you would sit down," she said in a soft, pretty, sympathetic way. "You have been so much troubled that you are very tired, and you need all your strength."

It was just as new to him to be spoken to and cared for in that gentle, simple way as it was to be contradicted. He was reminded of "the boy" again, and he actually did as she asked him. Perhaps his disappointment and wretchedness were good discipline for him; if he had not been wretched he might have continued to hate her, but just at present he found her a little soothing. She had so sweet a face and voice, and a pretty dignity when she spoke or moved. Very soon, by the quiet magic of these influences, he began to feel less gloomy, and then he talked still more.

"Whatever happens," he said, "the boy shall be provided for. He shall be taken care of, now and in the future."

Before he went away, he glanced around the room.

"Do you like the house?" he demanded.

"Very much," she answered.

"This is a cheerful room," he said. "May I come here again and talk this matter over?"

"As often as you wish, my lord," she replied.

And then he went out to his carriage and drove away, Thomas and Henry almost stricken dumb upon the box at the turn affairs had taken.

CHAPTER XIII.

DICK TO THE RESCUE.

Of course, as soon as the story of Lord Fauntleroy and the difficulties of the Earl of Dorincourt were discussed in the English newspapers, they were discussed in the American newspapers. The story was too interesting to be passed over lightly, and it was talked of a great deal. There were so many versions of it that it would have been an edifying thing to buy all the papers and compare them. Mr. Hobbs used to read the papers until his head was in a whirl, and in the evening he and Dick would talk it all over. They found out what an important personage an Earl of Dorincourt was, and what a magnificent income he possessed, and how many estates he owned, and how stately and beautiful was the Castle in which he lived; and the more they learned the more excited they became.

"Seem's like somethin' orter be done," said Mr. Hobbs.

But there really was nothing they could do but each write a letter to Cedric, containing assurances of their friendship and sympathy. They wrote those letters as soon as they could after receiving the news.

The very next morning, one of Dick's customers was rather surprised. He was a young lawyer just beginning practice; as poor as a very young lawyer can possibly be, but a bright, energetic young fellow, with sharp wit and a good temper. He had a shabby office near Dick's stand, and every morning Dick blacked his boots for him.

That particular morning, when he put his foot on the rest, he had an illustrated paper in his hand—an enterprising paper, with pictures in it of conspicuous people and things. He had just finished looking it over, and when the last boot was polished, he handed it to the boy.

"Here's a paper for you, Dick," he said. "Picture of an English castle in it and an English earl's daughter-in-law. You ought to become familiar with the nobility and gentry, Dick. Begin on the Right Honourable the Earl of Dorincourt and Lady Fauntleroy. Hello! I say, what's the matter?"

The pictures he spoke of were on the front page, and Dick was staring at one of them with his eyes and mouth open, and his sharp face almost pale with excitement.

He pointed to the picture, under which was written:

"Mother of Claimant (Lord Fauntleroy)."

It was the picture of a handsome woman, with large eyes and heavy braids of black hair wound around her head.

"Her!" said Dick. "I know her better'n I know you! An' I've struck work for this mornin'."

And in less than five minutes from that time he was tearing through the streets on his way to Mr. Hobbs and the corner store. Mr. Hobbs could scarcely believe the evidence of his senses when he looked across the counter and saw Dick rush in with the paper in his hand. The boy was out of breath with running; so much out of breath, in fact, that he could scarcely speak as he threw the paper down on the counter.

"Look at it!" panted Dick. "Look at that woman in the picture! That's what you look at! She aint no 'ristocrat, she aint!" with withering scorn. "She's no lord's wife. You may eat me, if it aint Minna—Minna! I'd know her anywheres, an' so'd Ben. Jest ax him."

Mr. Hobbs dropped into his seat.

"I knowed it was a put-up job," he said. "I knowed it; and they done it on account o' him bein' a 'Merican!"

"Done it!" cried Dick, with disgust. "She done it, that's who done it. I'll tell yer wot come to me, the minnit I saw her pictur. There was one o' them papers we saw had a letter in it that said somethin' 'bout her boy, an' it said he had a scar on his chin. Put them together—her 'n' that scar! Why that boy o' hers aint no more a lord than I am! It's Ben's boy."

Professor Dick Tipton had always been a sharp boy, and earning his living in the streets of a big city had made him still sharper. He had learned to keep his eyes open and his wits about him, and it mast be confessed he enjoyed immensely the excitement and impatience of that moment.

Mr. Hobbs was almost overwhelmed by his sense of responsibility, and Dick was all alive and full of energy. He began to write a letter to Ben, and he cut out the picture and inclosed it to him, and Mr. Hobbs wrote a letter to Cedric and one to the Earl. They were in the midst of this letter-writing when a new idea came to Dick.

"Say," he said, "the feller that give me the paper, he's a lawyer. Let's ax him what we'd better do. Lawyers knows it all."

Mr. Hobbs was immensely impressed by this suggestion and Dick's business capacity.

"That's so!" he replied. "This here calls for lawyers."

And leaving the store in care of a substitute, he struggled into his coat and marched down town with Dick, and the two presented themselves with their romantic story in Mr. Harrison's office, much to that young man's astonishment.

If he had not been a very young lawyer, with a very enterprising mind and a great deal of spare time on his hands, he might not have been so readily interested in what they had to say, for it all certainly sounded very wild and queer; but he chanced to want something to do very much.

"And," said Mr. Hobbs, "say what your time's worth an hour and look into this thing thorough, and I'll pay the damage—Silas Hobbs, corner of Blank Street, Vegetables and Groceries."

"Well," said Mr. Harrison, "it will be a big thing if it turns out all right, and it will be almost as big a thing for me as for Lord Fauntleroy; and at any rate, no harm can be done by investigating. It appears there has been some dubiousness about the child. The woman contradicted herself in some of her statements about his age, and aroused suspicion. The first persons to be written to are Dick's brother and the Earl of Dorincourt's family lawyer."

And actually before the sun went down, two letters had been written and sent in two different directions—one speeding out of New York harbour on a mail steamer on its way to England, and the other on a train carrying letters and passengers bound for California. And the first was addressed to T. Havisham, Esq., and the second to Benjamin Tipton.

And after the store was closed that evening, Mr. Hobbs and Dick sat in the back room and talked together until midnight.

CHAPTER XIV.

THE EXPOSURE.

It is astonishing how short a time it takes for very wonderful things to happen. It had taken only a few minutes, apparently, to change all the fortunes of the little boy dangling his red legs from the high stool in Mr. Hobbs's store, and to transform him from a small boy, living the simplest life in a quiet street, into an English nobleman, the heir to an earldom and magnificent wealth. It had taken only a few minutes, apparently, to change him from an English nobleman into a penniless little impostor, with no right to any of the splendours he had been enjoying. And, surprising as it may appear, it did not take nearly so long a time as one might have expected to alter the face of everything again and to give back to him all that he had been in danger of losing.

It took the less time because, after all, the woman who had called herself Lady Fauntleroy was not nearly so clever as she was wicked; and when she had been closely pressed by Mr. Havisham's questions about her marriage and her boy, she had made one or two blunders which had caused suspicion to be awakened; and then she had lost her presence of mind and her temper, and in her excitement and anger had betrayed herself still further. There seemed no doubt that she had been married to Bevis, Lord Fauntleroy, but Mr. Havisham found out that her story of the boy's being born in a certain part of London was false; and just when they all were in the midst of the commotion caused by this discovery, there came the letter from the young lawyer in New York, and Mr. Hobbs's letters also.

What an evening it was when those letters arrived, and when Mr. Havisham and the Earl sat and talked their plans over in the library!

"After my first three meetings with her," said Mr. Havisham, "I began to suspect her strongly. Our best plan will be to cable at once for these two Tiptons, say nothing about them to her, and suddenly confront her with them when she is not expecting it. My opinion is that she will betray herself on the spot."

And that was what actually happened. She was told nothing, but one fine morning, as she sat in her sitting-room at the inn called "The Dorincourt Arms," making some very fine plans for herself, Mr. Havisham was announced; and when he entered, he was followed by no leas than three persons—one was a sharp-faced boy and one was a big young man, and the third was the Earl of Dorincourt.

She sprang to her feet and actually uttered a cry of terror. She had thought of these new-comers as being thousands of miles away, when she had ever thought of them at all, which she had scarcely done for years. She had never expected to see them again. It must be confessed that Dick grinned a little when he saw her.

"Hello, Minna!" he said,

The big young man—who was Ben—stood still a minute and looked at her.

"Do you know her?" Mr. Havisham asked, glancing from one to the other.

"Yes," said Ben. "I know her and she knows me. I can swear to her in any court, and I can bring a dozen others who will. Her father is a respectable sort of man, and he's honest enough to be ashamed of her. He'll tell you who she is, and whether she married me or not."

Then he clenched his hand suddenly and turned on her.

"Where's the child?" he demanded. "He's going with me! He is done with you, and so am I!"

And just as he finished saying the words, the door leading into the bedroom opened a little, and the boy, probably attracted by the sound of the loud voices, looked in. He was not a handsome boy, but he had rather a nice face, and he was quite like Ben, his father, as any one could see, and there was the three-cornered scar on his chin.

Ben walked up to him and took his hand, and his own was trembling.

"Tom," he said to the little fellow. "I'm your father; I've come to take you away. Where's your hat?"

The boy pointed to where it lay on a chair. It evidently rather pleased him to hear that he was going away. Ben took up the hat and marched to the door.

"If you want me again," he said to Mr. Havisham, "you know where to find me."

He walked out of the room, holding the child's hand and not looking at the woman once. She was fairly raving with fury, and the Earl was calmly gazing at her through his eyeglasses, which he had quietly placed upon his aristocratic eagle nose.

"Come, come, my young woman," said Mr. Havisham. "This won't do at all. If you don't want to be locked up, you really must behave yourself."

And there was something so very business-like in his tones that, probably feeling that the safest thing she could do would be to get out of the way, she gave him one savage look and dashed past him into the next room and slammed the door.

"We shall have no more trouble with her," said Mr. Havisham.

And he was right; for that very night she left the Dorincourt Arms and took the train to London, and was seen no more.

When the Earl left the room after the interview, he went at once to his carriage.

"To Court Lodge," he said to Thomas.

"To Court Lodge," said Thomas to the coachman as he mounted the box; "an' you may depend on it, things is taking a uniggspected turn."

When the carriage stopped at Court Lodge, Cedric was in the drawing-room with his mother.

The Earl came in without being announced. He looked an inch or so taller, and a great many years younger. His deep eyes flashed.

"Where," he said, "is Lord Fauntleroy?"

Mrs. Errol came forward, a flush rising to her cheek.

"Is it Lord Fauntleroy?" she asked. "Is it, indeed?"

The Earl put out his hand and grasped hers.

"Yes," he answered, "it is."

Then he put his other hand on Cedric's shoulder.

"Fauntleroy," he said in his unceremonious, authoritative way, "ask your mother when she will come to us at the Castle."

Fauntleroy flung his arms around his mother's neck.

"To live with us!" he cried. "To live with us always!"

The Earl looked at Mrs. Errol, and Mrs. Errol looked at the Earl. His lordship was entirely in earnest. He had made up his mind to waste no time in arranging this matter. He had begun to think it would suit him to make friends with his heir's mother.

"Are you quite sure you want me?" said Mrs. Errol, with her soft, pretty smile.

"Quite sure," he said bluntly. "We have always wanted you, but we were not exactly aware of it. We hope you will come."

CHAPTER XV.

HIS EIGHTH BIRTHDAY.

Ben took his boy and went back to his cattle ranch in California, and he returned under very comfortable circumstances. Just before his going, Mr. Havisham had an interview with him in which the lawyer told him that the Earl of Dorincourt wished to do something for the boy who might have turned out to be Lord Fauntleroy. And so when Ben went away, he went as the prospective master of a ranch which would be almost as good as his own, and might easily become his own in time, as indeed it did in the course of a few years; and Tom, the boy, grew up on it into a fine young man and was devotedly fond of his father; and they were so successful and happy that Ben used to say that Tom made up to him for all the troubles he had ever had.

But Dick and Mr. Hobbs—who had actually come over with the others to see that things were properly looked after—did not return for some time. It had been decided at the outset that the Earl would provide for Dick, and would see that he received a solid education; and Mr. Hobbs had decided that as he himself had left a reliable substitute in charge of his store, he could afford to wait to see the festivities which were to celebrate Lord Fauntleroy's eighth birthday. All the tenantry were invited, and there were to be feasting and dancing and games in the park, and bonfires and fireworks in the evening.

"Just like the Fourth of July!" said Lord Fauntleroy. "It seems a pity my birthday wasn't on the Fourth, doesn't it? For then we could keep them both together."

What a grand day it was when little Lord Fauntleroy's birthday arrived, and how his young lordship enjoyed it! How beautiful the park looked, filled with the thronging people dressed in their gayest and best, and with the flags flying from the tents and the top of the Castle! Nobody had stayed away who could possibly come, because everybody was really glad that little Lord Fauntleroy was to be little Lord Fauntleroy still, and some day was to be the master of everything. Every one wanted to have a look at him, and at his pretty, kind mother, who had made so many friends.

What scores and scores of people there were under the trees, and in the tents, and on the lawns! Farmers and farmers' wives in their Sunday suits and bonnets and shawls; children frolicking and chasing about; and old dames in red cloaks gossiping together. At the Castle, there were ladies and gentlemen who had come to see the fun, and to congratulate the Earl, and to meet Mrs. Errol. Lady Lorridaile and Sir Harry were there, and Mr. Havisham, of course.

Everybody looked after little Lord Fauntleroy. And the sun shone and the flags fluttered and the games were played and the dances danced, and as the gaieties went on and the joyous afternoon passed, his little lordship was simply radiantly happy.

The whole world seemed beautiful to him.

There was some one else who was happy too,—an old man, who, though he had been rich and noble all his life, had not often been very honestly happy. Perhaps, indeed, I shall tell you that I think it was because he was rather better than he had been that he was rather happier. He had not, indeed, suddenly become as good as Fauntleroy thought him; but, at least, he had begun to love something, and he had several times found a sort of pleasure in doing the kind things which the innocent, kind little heart of a child had suggested,—and that was a beginning. And every day he had been more pleased with his son's wife. He liked to hear her sweet voice and to see her sweet face; and as she sat in his arm-chair, he used to watch her and listen as he talked to her boy; and he heard loving, gentle words which were new to him, and he began to see why the little fellow who had lived in a New York side street and known grocery-men and made friends with boot-blacks, was still so well-bred and manly a little fellow that he made no one ashamed of him, even when fortune changed him into the heir to an English earldom, living in an English castle.

As the old Earl of Dorincourt looked at him that day, moving about the park among the people, talking to those he knew and making his ready little bow when any one greeted him, entertaining his friends Dick and Mr. Hobbs, or standing near his mother listening to their conversation, the old nobleman was very well satisfied with him. And he had never been better satisfied than he was when they went down to the biggest tent, where the more important tenants of the Dorincourt estate were sitting down to the grand collation of the day.

They were drinking toasts; and, after they had drunk the health of the Earl with much more enthusiasm than his name had ever been greeted with before, they proposed the health of "Little Lord Fauntleroy." And if there had ever been any doubt at all as to whether his lordship was popular or not, it would have been settled that instant. Such a clamour of voices and such a rattle of glasses and applause!

Little Lord Fauntleroy was delighted. He stood and smiled, and made bows, and flushed rosy red with pleasure up to the roots of his bright hair.

"Is it because they like me, Dearest?" he said to his mother. "Is it Dearest? I'm so glad!"

And then the Earl put his hand on the child's shoulder and said to him:

"Fauntleroy, say to them that you thank them for their kindness."

Fauntleroy gave a glance up at him and then at his mother.

"Must I?" he asked just a trifle shyly, and she smiled, and nodded. And so he made a little step forward, and everybody looked at him—such a beautiful, innocent little fellow he was, too, with his brave, trustful face!—and he spoke as loudly as he could, his childish voice ringing out quite clear and strong.

"I'm ever so much obliged to you!" he said, "and—I hope you'll enjoy my birthday—because I've enjoyed it so much—and—I'm very glad I'm going to be an earl—I didn't think at first I should like it, but now I do—and I love this place so, and I think it is beautiful—and—and—and when I am an earl, I am going to try to be as good as my grandfather."

And amid the shouts and clamour of applause, he stepped back with a little sigh of relief, and put his hand into the Earl's and stood close to him, smiling and leaning against his side.

And that would be the very end of my story; but I must add one curious piece of information, which is that Mr. Hobbs became so fascinated with high life and was so reluctant to leave his young friend that he actually sold his corner store in New York, and settled in the English village of Erlesboro, where he opened a shop which was patronized by the Castle and consequently was a great success. And about ten years after, when Dick, who had finished his education and was going to visit his brother in California, asked the good grocer if he did not wish to return to America, he shook his head seriously.

"Not to live there," he said. "Not to live there; I want to be near him. It's a good enough country for them that's young an stirrin'—but there's faults in it. There's not an auntsister among 'em—nor an earl!"

THE END